STAR DUST AND THE BILLIONAIRE

BILLIONAIRE LONELY HEARTS CLUB BOOK TWO

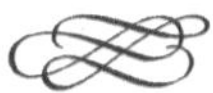

EDITH MACKENZIE

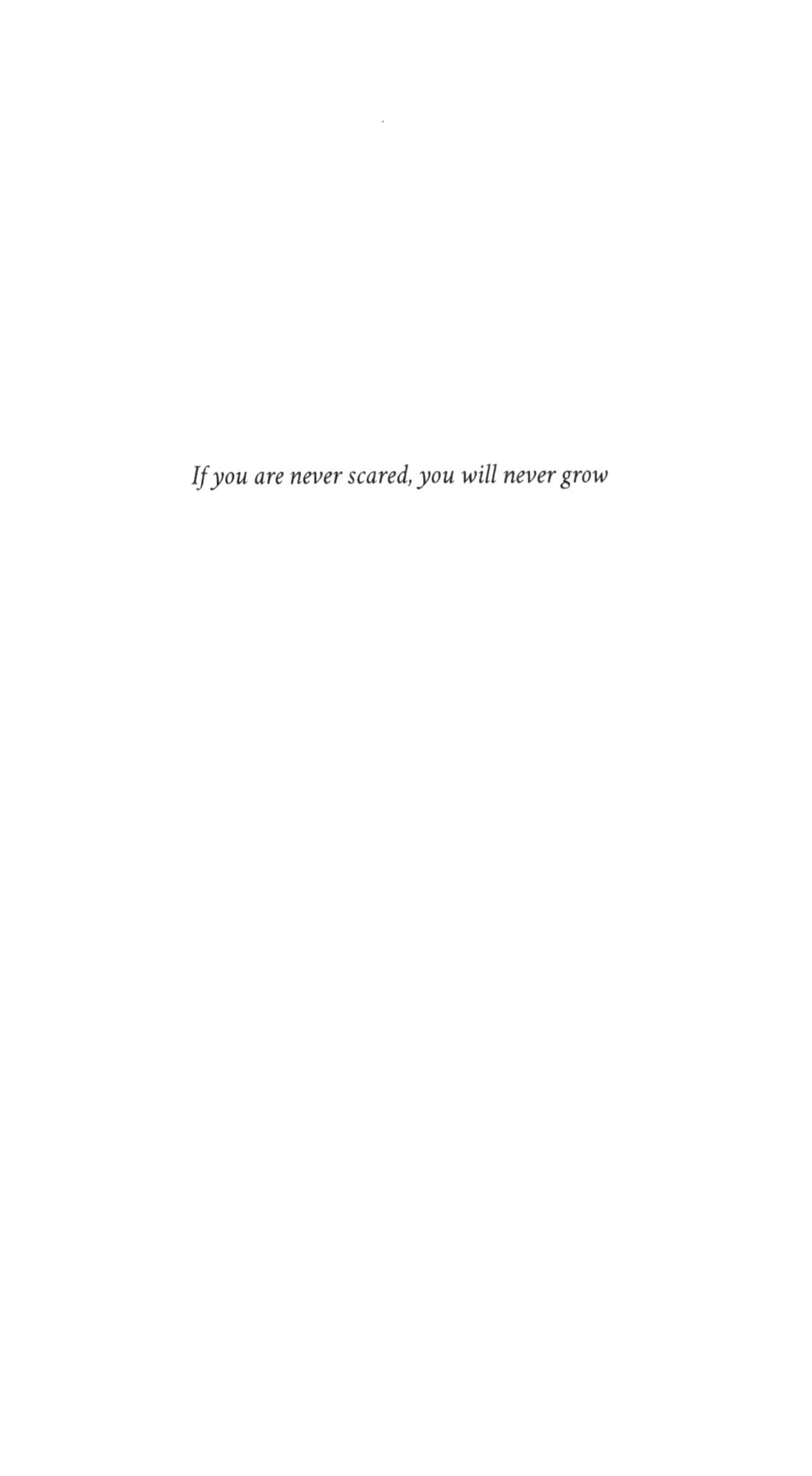

If you are never scared, you will never grow

CHAPTER 1

She didn't belong. That was Stirling's first impression when he saw her tucked into a corner doing her best to make herself appear invisible. Given the striking skintight red dress she was wearing, that was going to be next to impossible. Already a few members of the club were eyeing her with interest. The red she wore was a power color and one of passion, and her heels were sky high. And yet, it seemed at odds with the way she tugged at her hemline and adjusted her glasses as she peered around as if waiting for someone. *Lucky guy.* She looked down, tapping away on her phone, her face hidden by her shoulder-length ash-blonde hair.

She was a tantalizing prospect, and one he fully intended to investigate further. "Are you listening at all?" his friend demanded. It wasn't like Freddy to get so upset, but then again, his sister wasn't listening to reason about her boyfriend. It made Stirling thankful he was an only child—much easier that way.

"No, old boy." He waved for another glass of scotch. "I

must admit I wasn't paying the least bit of attention. I was somewhat distracted."

Freddy followed his line of gaze. "I've never seen her here before, and I'd remember if I had."

"Well, I'm about to make her acquaintance."

"You'd better hurry before someone else beats you to it. They're already circling. I think I'll give Bella another call and see if she wants to come out."

"Do you really want her boyfriend here? And if he's out of town, there's no way his goons will let her out alone."

Freddy's face soured as he took a drink. "I know, but I've got to try." He nodded toward the vision in red. "Good luck."

Smiling at the thrill of the upcoming chase, Stirling rose. "Luck has nothing to do with it. Not if you're working with what I am."

"A large ego?"

"It helps. So does being quite the billionaire catch." Hooking them was easy, it was trying to release them back into the wild afterwards that was the difficult part. "Good luck with Bella, too. She's lucky she has a brother who cares."

"Thanks, Stirling. You'd better hurry. It looks like someone is going to beat you to your lady."

Not needing further urging, he was gone. Little Red was in for quite the night.

Maybe red hadn't been the best outfit choice if she wanted to blend in, especially one that required copious amounts of Hollywood tape just to protect her modesty. But there'd been something about it that had made her feel glamourous and special. Pausing from taking her notes, Cassie pushed her glasses back up the bridge of her nose. *I wonder if this is what an investigative journalist feels like—a little dangerous and a*

whole lot of fun. She blinked. Why was the incredibly handsome man eyeballing her? She quickly peeked over her shoulder just to be sure there wasn't some tall glamourous blonde behind her. Nope. He was definitely still looking her way. Panic set a fluttering in her belly as he rose, still holding her eye, a deliberateness to him as he adjusted his cufflinks and the slight tilt of his head as he said something to his friend before sauntering her way. Maybe she wouldn't be feeling so lightheaded if she'd been able to eat anything before she'd left for her little investigative foray. *Dang dress.* A slight shiver ran through her. It felt like she was being stalked by the Big Bad Wolf.

"Hi, babe, I got this for you."

A champagne flute thrust into her line of vision caused Cassie to jerk back. She stared incredulously at the short man who had materialized beside her. *Where on earth had he come from?*

"I think you'll find that the lady isn't interested in your Champagne," the Big Bad Wolf said, his voice low and rumbling. *Even his voice is sexy.* He gestured to the bartender. "The lady will have"—he paused, insolently looking her up and down—"a martini."

"The lady already has a drink," insisted her short-statured suitor.

"I think you'll find the lady would prefer something a little headier." The Big Bad Wolf gave her a slow wink. "Am I right?"

Geeze, this guy was one arrogant so-and-so, but wasn't that the kind of guy she was hoping to meet here? He would be perfect for her purposes. Giving him her best flirtatious look—the one she'd been practicing in her mirror all week—Cassie smiled. "Sounds perfect."

～

IT REALLY WAS DISAPPOINTING how easily she'd been caught. He'd wanted the little minx in glasses and a red dress to be different from the rest. Staring his competition off, he gave her a smug half smile. "Well, Little Red, do you have a name?"

"Isn't it usually polite to introduce yourself before asking a lady her name?" She arched a brow at him reproachfully.

Hmm, a little fire there. Interesting. Maybe she wasn't as meek as he'd assumed and was, judging from the accent, American. "My mother would have me for my poor manners. Please accept my most humble apologies. I am Stirling Saint-Claire. You may have heard of me?" He held out the martini to her.

At least she had the decency to not play coy, recognition blooming on her face as she accepted her drink from him. "The movie producer?"

"One and the same. Now, Little Red, I believe it's your turn to give me your name."

"I'm Cassie. Well, Cassandra Pearson." She peered at him from underneath dark lashes.

Stirling had the unsettling sensation that she was watching to see if he recognized the name. It didn't ring any bells for him, and he was sure he'd remember her if they'd previously had a dalliance. "Well, Cassie, since you appear to know all about me, what do you do?"

Her hazel eyes narrowed ever so slightly, as if trying to decide how to answer. *Surely it wasn't that difficult of a question.* "I'm an author."

"Really? I quite enjoy reading myself. Mainly these days it's scripts, but I still read the odd book when I get the chance. Would I know anything you've written, or are you one of those indie authors who seem to think they are taking over the publishing world?"

Cassie's nostrils flared. "Actually, I'm a New York Bestselling Author and I just so happen to be one of those indie authors as well."

"Good for you. I like seeing people get ahead."

A muscle twitched in her jaw. "Which you should know, considering your production company optioned one of my books."

"We did?" The earlier disappointment returned with a vengeance. So, she was just here to make sure her book went further than the option stage. He had to give it to her, she was resourceful tracking him down to his club. He'd never had an author do that before. "Well then, let me have it. Why should I take your book further and make it into a film?"

Her jaw worked as she glared at him from narrowed eyes. "Excuse me?" There was a strangled quality to her voice, like she was barely maintaining control. "The book speaks for itself both in quality and the sheer number of sales it's had." Cassie forcefully set the half-finished martini onto the bar. "Thanks for the drink, but I didn't come here to be insulted."

So, now she wanted to play coy. "I don't understand how you've been insulted. You did go to a lot of effort to come here and get my attention and now you have it." He gave her a slow steady appraisal again. He really did appreciate how good she looked in that little red dress. "So go on, give me your best elevator pitch."

Cassie drew herself up to her full height, which did all sorts of interesting things to the curves being contained by that dress. "Excuse me?" Stirling stifled a smile. She was puffing up like an irate bantam hen, and he'd never seen anything hotter in his life. "I did not come here to get your attention. In fact, getting your attention was the absolutely last thing I wanted from tonight, or any night for that matter."

He wet his bottom lip, enjoying the way she bristled when

he smiled lazily at her. "Then pray tell, why did you come here looking like that if you didn't want my attention?"

"Because I need to research my next book and it's none of your business what I look like. You didn't even know me until five minutes ago."

"Actually, as you said so yourself, I've known you since I optioned your book."

"Which you didn't know anything about since some assistant probably took care of it all."

"Details." He waved her protest aside, enjoying the high color flooding her cheeks. The way she bit—he hadn't had so much fun in a long time. "You've intrigued me. What is your next book about that you need to research it?"

"It's about billionaires, if you must know," she ground out. Stirling thought she might actually be on the verge of stamping her foot.

"Well, you're in luck, since I just so happen to be one. What do you want to know, sweetheart?"

CHAPTER 2

Cassie was at war with herself as she bit down on her lower lip. His high-handed manner both excited and annoyed her. One thing was for sure—Stirling Saint-Claire had an ego bigger than Texas and might just be what she was looking for. That is, if she could overcome her irritation at what seemed to appear to be his habitual smugness.

The plan had been relatively simple. Somehow sweet talk her way into the most exclusive members' club in London. *Because obviously there was something quite classy and sexy about an English billionaire.* Or at least that's what she'd thought when she'd created her love interest for her latest romance. She was rapidly beginning to think English billionaires were much better suited to being the antagonist in any plot. So far, getting in had been the easy part. A few discreet inquiries, a little harmless flirting and a promise not to cause any trouble or name names, and before she'd known it, she'd had a front row seat at the bar to start taking notes. That was until the arrogant Big Bad Wolf had decided to thrust himself upon her.

Cassie sucked on the inside of her cheek. *Maybe this guy was a little too much to handle. Best to throw him back and try for a smaller, less intimidating fish.* "I don't think you'll be able to help me."

"Why on earth not?" The accent that could only have been the result of years of good breeding didn't falter once as he regarded her as one would a simpleton. "Is it quantum physics? I did dabble a little at Cambridge, but I am more versed in Ancient Civilizations thanks to always listening to my friend Landon drone on and on about them. I mean, sometimes when I'm having trouble falling asleep, I think about what Landon would say and I nod off just like that." Stirling snapped his fingers together.

They were nice strong fingers, Cassie noticed. Shaking her head, she tried not to let herself get distracted. "No, it's not about that."

"How about wild horses in the Australian outback? I know a thing or two about them now."

Cassie pulled her glasses down slightly as she rubbed the bridge of her nose. Why couldn't the man just get the hint and leave her alone? Wasn't that what she wanted? "Will you just stop? It's a romance, okay?"

His look turned purely masculine and very sexy. The Big Bad Wolf was out in full force. "I know a thing or two about that as well."

Cassie tried to ignore the warmth she could feel creeping up her neck and spilling onto her cheeks. Coolly, she stared at him. "Well, I'm not asking you."

That look—the I-know-you're-playing-hard-to-get-and-I-like-it look—stared back at her. "You came here to research, isn't that what you just told me?"

"Yes."

"Well, you found a willing subject." He gave her a courtly bow. "I put myself entirely at your disposal."

She imposed an iron control on herself, forbidding her blush to deepen. Taking a step forward, Cassie made a show of looking him over, which wasn't hard considering his arresting good looks and commanding presence had completely captured her attention. His smile broadened under her gaze.

"I'm here to research the main love interest, but I guess every story needs a villain." She smiled sweetly at him. "I don't see why the spurned lover can't be an English billionaire, too."

If anything, her words seemed to amuse him. *What was it going to take for him to leave her alone?* "Excuse me, miss, can I please see your membership?" An efficient man appeared at her side. He wasn't one of the staff members who had helped her gain access.

"I seem to have misplaced it." Cassie tried to appear unconcerned while inside she was fuming. It was all this jerk's fault for drawing too much attention to her.

"If you can't produce it, you'll have to come with me."

"She's with me." The attendant's manner immediately changed at Stirling's coolly superior tone.

I didn't expect that. But the way he'd taken control, like he could snap his fingers and everyone would fall into line, got on Cassie's nerves. Even though she knew she was cutting off her nose to spite her face, she plunged on. "Actually, I'd rather get thrown out than have anyone think I was with you." Spinning dramatically on her high heels, she channeled every New York Queen she'd ever seen in a club and sashayed her way out, leaving the attendant and Stirling to stare in her wake. *Take that.*

THE LEATHER of the couch creaked as Stirling placed his hands behind his head and leaned back, enjoying the view his corner office provided out over London as he rested a foot on the polished glass coffee table in front of him. When home in England, he found that he couldn't fight against the need to have restrained displays of wealth. The best materials, location, and neighbors, but nothing too ostentatious—he saved that for LA. Stretched out comfortably, he closed his eyes, opening his mind up and allowing it to drift. It was a practice he tried to do every day, a mindfulness that allowed him to center himself. Today it centered solely on the previous evening—and hadn't it delivered. One tantalizing feisty little minx, to be exact, before she was snatched from his grasp. A pity. She'd been rather fun with all her hissing and side glances. His foot slid from the table as a hazy memory swam languidly up from the depths of his mind. Hadn't she mentioned something about him having an option on one of her books?

Stirling touched a button beside him. "Angie, can you please come in?"

His finger had barely left the hard plastic before his assistant materialized like some well-groomed wraith. "Yes, Mr Saint-Claire?"

"I need you to find out everything you can about one Cassandra Pearson, and I believe the best place to start is with a book we have optioned of hers."

"Is there anything in particular you're looking for?" Stirling had to give it to Angie. Not much surprised her and she was very thorough.

"I want everything there is to know about her."

His assistant didn't even twitch. "Very well, Mr Saint-Claire. I'll have some preliminary findings for you by the end of the day."

"Excellent." Stirling closed his eyes to the sound of the door softly closing. *There was more than one way to skin a feisty red cat.* Anticipation thrummed through him. *The chase was back on.*

CHAPTER 3

*H*is hands were beautiful, long-fingered and strong.
*Odd that she should notice them when he'd carried
himself with such a commanding air of self-confidence as he stood
in front of her looking devilishly handsome. Samantha froze,
caught between a volatile cocktail of emotions as he lazily looked
her up and down. "The lady wants a martini," he said in a posh
English accent.*

"For the love of God!"

Cassie angrily pushed her keyboard away. Unbelievable. The jerk from last night was still bothering her, forcing himself into her writing. The nerve of the man! Tapping her foot, she tried to picture her romantic interest. Tall, an air to him that only the truly wealthy and privilege had, a dangerous air, like the Big Bad Wolf. *That's it, this is getting ridiculous.* Snatching her bag from the couch beside her, she stormed out of her rented studio apartment. Maybe it was time to do some more research, freshen up some details in her mind. After all, she had to make the most of her time in London before she had to fly back to LA. Maybe it was time to see what the girlfriend of a billionaire did to fill her days.

CASSIE HAD to fight the urge to turn around and head straight back home. The first shop was a disaster. The impossibly tall and thin sales assistant took one look at her and, as if possessing x-ray vision and seeing the contents of her purse, snidely commented that the thrift shop was several streets over. Humiliated, Cassie slunk from the premises with her tail between her legs. Regrouping on the sidewalk and spying a high-end boutique whose creations she'd always loved, she decided that one didn't falter at the first hurdle. Pulling her hair loose, she tugged her scarf up to partially cover her face. Between that and her oversized sunglasses, she hoped to give off just the right mysterious air of a celebrity, or at least enough that they wouldn't throw her out on the spot.

Turns out it wasn't a look she could pull off, although it did get the attention of the sales assistant that followed her around and, with a loud clearing of their throat, warned her from touching anything if she so much as looked at it. *What a bunch of stuck-up wannabes.* Head high in the air, she marched across the polished concrete floor, the hard eyes of the woman tracking her every move.

"This is all so last year anyway," Cassie loudly declared as once again she exited out onto the pavement. *I am so done with today.*

"Hello, Little Red." The voice was unmistakable. *Like, really really done with today.*

With a deliberately casual move, she turned to face the last person she wanted to see in that moment. The devilish gleam of amusement in his eyes was almost her undoing. "I have a name, but I'm sure you don't remember it."

"Cassandra Pearson. New York Times Bestselling Author of such series as *The Love of a Cowboy, Everything is Bigger in*

Texas and *The Cat Nanny Diaries*. I believe it's the *War Brides* series that we optioned."

"Look who knows how to do internet research." Sarcasm dripped from every word as she folded her arms across her chest. *Seriously, this man.*

"Well, not me, obviously. But my assistant does."

"I should have known you would get someone else to do your dirty work."

He gave her a heavy-lidded smirk. "I rather enjoy—" He sucked in his bottom lip as his stared at her. Cassie's heart almost pounded from her chest. "—getting my hands dirty. For the right cause, that is. Now, Little Red, we can continue to stand here, or you can let me take you to a rather nice eatery just down the way."

"I don't think I need to keep you from whatever it is you were doing here."

She wanted to punch that look right off his face. "What do you think I'm doing here?"

"I just assumed you were buying something lacy and skimpy for your latest paramour." No doubt it would be something incredibly expensive that whispered softly against the skin. Cassie shivered.

A knowing gleam lit his eyes. Cassie wished he would quit looking at her like he knew exactly how he was affecting her. "Jealous?"

"Why would I be jealous?" *The nerve of the man.*

"Because you wish it was you." Cassie spluttered at the sheer arrogance of the Englishman. "Rest easy, Little Red, I'm single." Stirling leaned in closer. "And you have my full atten-tion." His breath was warm against her ear. He straightened suddenly, leaving Cassie feeling completely unbalanced. "Now, I have an offer for you, and I think it would be worth your while to hear it."

She bit down hard on her bottom lip as she considered

her options. What did she really have to lose by finding out what he had to say? *Only my last shred of sanity.* "Fine."

Stirling gave her a lazy smile like he hadn't been expecting any other reply. One day he was going to be in for one heck of a surprise when someone didn't do what he wanted. Cassie hoped she was around to see it or, better still, was the one to deliver the unpleasant experience.

Before long she found herself seated at a white covered table, everything understated in only the way the rich liked it. Stirling sat easily, a man completely at home in his surroundings as the waiter presented him with a wine list. Making a selection, he quickly ordered food for both of them. Cassie's nostrils flared at his high-handed manner. She also suspected that what he ordered wasn't on the menu—just another thing the wealthy expected. She made a mental note to add it to her book.

Resting a hand lightly on the table, his Rolex glinting in the light, he turned the full force of his attention to her. "Last night you mentioned you were doing research for your new book on billionaires. How's it going?"

Cassie snorted. "Well, since I've met you, I've been kicked out of an exclusive members' club, and even the shop attendants think I'm invisible, or at the very least should be shopping at charity stores."

"I could see that being an issue."

She glared at him, unsure if he'd just insulted her or was commiserating. "What do you mean by that?"

"Pardon me for being blunt, but you haven't the look of money."

Cassie's mouth compressed into a thin line. "Excuse me? This isn't exactly a Walmart outfit."

"Yes, but it also isn't Chanel. Money recognizes money. It opens doors. And if you don't have it, those doors will remain closed to you. You're already seeing that for yourself."

"So, you invited me here to make fun of me? Rub my face in my failure by telling me I look poor?" Cassie picked her bag up, preparing to leave. "I'll have you know, I'm far from finished. Are all rich people such judgmental snobs?" She looked around. "Will your reputation survive being seen with poor little old me?"

Stirling gave a hearty chuckle. *Even the man's laugh was sexy.* "I think my reputation is safe. And I didn't invite you here to make fun of you. I have my own reasons."

"And they are?"

Heat fanned through her at his smoldering look. "I find you rather intriguing and there aren't many people I can honestly say that about. I'm suggesting that I pose as your boyfriend."

Cassie opened her mouth and closed it again, staring at him like he'd lost his mind. "Why on earth would you do that? And better still, why would I agree?"

"It will get my parents off my back, since all my friends keep getting married and they can't remember the last time I introduced a steady girlfriend to them."

"So, it's business then? But you didn't answer why I would agree to it."

"A little business, a little personal amusement. And you said yourself that you haven't exactly been successful with getting the research you need. If you're on my arm, all those doors that are firmly closed to you will magically open. You will see the billionaire lifestyle up close for yourself—the private planes, the houses, the private islands, the parties, the shopping, the people. I am the key to the billionaire kingdom, if you will."

"If you think I'm tempted by your offer, you've got a screw loose."

"I can already see you're tempted, and don't try to deny it.

Your mind is ticking over, thinking of all the juicy stuff you can discover and put in your story."

"No one will ever believe we're together." Even to her ears her voice sounded feeble, clutching at straws.

He flashed that infernal smug look of his again. "They will if I say we are."

Cassie chewed her bottom lip. Dang it all, he had her. She really did want to see it all, experience it for herself. She knew how much better her book would be if it felt authentic. "As long as you remember that it's all just pretend."

Stirling gave her a half smile. "Of course."

SHE'D MADE him work for it, there was no doubt about it. There had been some instances during their conversation where he'd suspected she wouldn't agree. Stirling had figured she'd be stubborn—it was part of her attraction—but Little Red was next level.

Light hazel eyes narrowed, bemused and opaque. "So, you just announce we're together and all these doors will magically open."

Stirling allowed himself an amused humph. "Of course not. You will attend several functions with me, and I'll take you shopping, make sure it's very obvious that I'm paying for everything. That should take care of getting the news out there that you are my new lady love. Believe me, those shop girls love to gossip, and that news will travel fast. This weekend we'll head over to the French Riviera and be seen out and about. You will drop into my London office, and I'll make sure to drop everything to see you. After that, we'll fly to LA due to my work commitments and be seen at all the hottest spots and industry events. Having you move into my Hollywood Hills mansion will certainly get the tongues wagging, since that's never happened before." He was actually looking forward to pranking most of his peers.

"But I only just got here. I flew all the way over to spend time here to research British billionaires and now you want me to just go back home again."

Trust her to protest even though she was getting exactly what she'd set out for. Stirling suspected it was her default setting. "Congratulations, you've hooked one, so I suggest you hang on and enjoy the ride.

CHAPTER 4

Stirling's hand hovered over the rows of cufflinks. His friends had made fun of his obsession with his appearance for years and he'd taken a little of the glamour of Hollywood and embraced it. His teeth had been straightened and whitened. Not the blinding, could-light-up-a-dark-road-in-the-middle-of-the-night treatment, but an improvement, nonetheless. It was the same with his wardrobe—each item needed to be custom tailored. Stirling didn't particularly care how much it cost. What he did care about was the fit and the quality that only a craftsman could provide. The navy suit he was wearing tonight was a prime example. Now for the final touches. *Ahh, perfect.* His hand lowered on the Cartier cufflinks, the jewels of the panther's eyes glowing. Lately he found that he had quite the affinity for cats. Stirling smiled in anticipation of the evening. *Would she be wearing red?* Securing his cuff, he grabbed a velvet case from the glass counter in his dressing room and strode from the room. *There was only one way to find out.*

Pewter gray. Sure, the dress was classy, elegant and sophisticated, but it wasn't his Little Red. Her shoes more than made up for it—electric blue high-heeled sandals with gold chains that dangled from the straps. Stirling offered his arm. "I wasn't sure you were going to show."

Dark lashes peeked over the rim of her glasses, framing offended hazel eyes. "What kind of girl stands up her pretend billionaire boyfriend?"

"One that doesn't let him pick her up for their date." Stirling liked that she hadn't capitulated easily into their fake relationship. "But you could have at least let me take you out for dinner."

"Do you know how hard it is to eat when you're wearing control panties?"

"No, and now I'm thinking about your undergarments." Two bright splashes of color appeared on her cheeks, her gaze darting away. Stirling was beginning to think she didn't mind his flirting as much as she made out. "For a man who's familiar with the female form, I don't believe you have to worry about them to wear a dress like that. Next time, leave them off and we can enjoy something to eat."

"How about we stop talking about what's under my dress and focus on what's important," she muttered, looking around as if looking for who might have overheard their conversation.

"I thought what we were talking about was important." He hadn't thought it was possible for the color on her face to deepen. Turns out he was wrong.

"Do you go to the theater often?" Stirling blinked at her change in topic. Fine, he would let it go for now.

"When I get a chance. Anything to do with performance, really. Theater, art house movies, ballet, even the odd Christmas pantomime."

"Have you always been drawn to creativity?" Cassie dropped slightly behind as they entered the building.

"Yes. I do believe my parents thought it was a phase, but to their credit, they have been supportive."

"It helps that you've been successful at it."

Stirling nodded at some of the patrons as he led her up the plushily carpeted steps toward the private boxes. "I believe it has helped, yes." He slipped a hand onto the small of her back as he guided her forward. "Smile. I do believe people are noticing the beautiful woman on my arm."

"Do you know them?" she whispered, tilting her face charmingly toward him.

"Yes, one is a reality TV star, another a Page Three girl. The man with them is a nightclub promoter. D-grade celebrities like that are the biggest gossips. I wouldn't be surprised if they haven't already posted it to their social media."

"Oh. I hadn't really thought about how famous people operated." Her brows were furrowed as she thought it over. "Is it always like that?"

"You need to think about it as two circles that overlap. One circle is celebrity, and one is wealth. Now, some wealthy people don't want anything to do with celebrities, and some celebrities don't want to be overshadowed by people who have more wealth and influence than they do. However, there is a lot of intermingling between the groups. My parents, for example, wouldn't even bother knowing the names of the people back there. They would consider them vulgar." He gestured for her to precede him into the box, untying the wine-colored velvet drapes behind them.

"But you know them." Cassie settled herself demurely into her chair, crossing her legs at the ankles.

"Of course. I have the wealth and position from my family name, but I have the power from being a movie producer to create or destroy a celebrity."

Cassie shifted her weight slightly away from him, there

was a pensive shimmer in the shadows of her eyes. "And do you enjoy that?"

Stirling gazed out over the audience, milling around as they found their seats. "No. I enjoy having power and what that brings me, but I've never used it against someone who didn't deserve it."

She pursed her lips as she gazed intently at him. "So, who do you consider as someone who deserves it?"

"The movie director who grooms young girls with the promise of stardom, for one." Approval shone from her brightly, and Stirling felt the knot in his stomach relax. "For what it's worth, I also make sure my leading lady is paid the same as my leading man."

"As long as you look after your authors when you make their books into films."

He reached into his coat pocket and extracted the velvet case, holding it out for her. "Will this do?"

Cassie stared down at it perplexedly before gazing up at him. Hesitantly, she took it from him and opened it. "Wow." Closing it, she handed it back.

"Don't you like it?" He had thought gold was a safe choice, but maybe she would have preferred the platinum.

"I've never seen anything so majestic in all my life, let alone hold it in my hands."

Stirling listened in dazed bewilderment. "Then why am I now holding it in my hands?"

"Because I didn't really think it was for me."

"Why would I give you something that wasn't for you?"

"Because I know how much that bracelet is worth. I actually researched it for one of my characters and it's not the sort of thing you buy for someone you just met." Her foot had begun to twitch during her tirade.

Stirling extracted the bracelet from its velvet prison, turning it around until the panther's emerald eyes flickered to life in the light of their private box. "It is, however, something a billionaire would get for his girlfriend."

"Pretend girlfriend."

"How are you going to do your research if you fight me every step of the way?" He held the diamond encrusted bracelet out to her. "Do you want to know what it's like to live the billionaire lifestyle or not?"

The white of her front teeth glistened as she nibbled on her bottom lip. Clearly Little Red was tempted. "But it's so expensive."

"That's the whole point. And not for me it isn't. That's what you need to remember. The amount of money I have its obscene. This"—he waggled the jewelry at her—"is just a trinket."

Cassie stared at it, longing plain on her face as she fought with her desire for the exquisite jewelry and her independent streak. "Fine." Her face softened into a smile. "I could say I'm only doing it because I'm researching, but we both know that's a lie. Thank you, it's gorgeous." Joyfully, she held her wrist out to him. "Would you please be so kind as to put it on for me?" Stirling was riveted as the bracelet encircled her slender wrist. The matching panthers on his cuffs winked in the light. "Oh," she said in a startled voice. "I didn't realize we were twins."

"Maybe it's my way of claiming you." Stirling spoke in a casual, jesting manner, though somehow the idea was incredibly satisfying.

A light giggle bubbled out of her. "I swear you're such a good actor you almost had me believing you. But you don't need to lay it on so thick." The lights dimmed as the crowd began to quieten in anticipation. "It's about to start," she said in her best stage whisper.

As far as Stirling was concerned, he'd much rather keep watching Cassie than any performer that was due to appear.

Noticing the rapt attention on her face, he sighed and stretched his legs out as the stage curtain rose. One couldn't really complain when coming to the theater had been his idea.

~

It most certainly hadn't been Cassie's first time to the theater. It was, however, the first time she'd been seated in a private box with a billionaire—a very complex and intriguing one at that. It hadn't taken long for her—long-time people watcher, part-time analyzer—to discover that the arrogance that Stirling wore like a mantle was only one aspect to his multifaceted personality. The glint of the panther's emerald eyes on her wrist drew her attention and she turned it to better marvel at the glamorous gift he'd chosen for her. *Maybe I'm giving him too much credit. It was probably his assistant who selected it. Or maybe he just has a box of expensive trinkets that he hands out like candy.* Somehow, and she didn't know why, she didn't think that was the case. This bracelet felt personal.

Rapturous applause exploded in the cinema, the curtains dramatically swishing closed before opening again to reveal the cast. "What did you think?" Warm amusement washed through his crisp English accent. Guiltily, Cassie covered the bracelet she'd been admiring with her hand. His fingers were warm and strong as they removed her hand, lifting the jewelry up to the light. "Don't be ashamed to admire beauty." He raised her hand to his lips, his eyes never leaving hers. "It's one of life's great pleasures."

He brushed a kiss gently to the delicate skin of her hand. For a moment, Cassie forgot how to breathe, electricity coursing through her from the contact. She swallowed, finding her mouth had suddenly turned into a desert. "I enjoyed the play."

"I enjoy our play, too." There was a simmering fire, a challenge in the way he looked at her.

"I said *the* play." Cassie felt the need to further expand. There was a dangerously intimate undertone to his words. "The play we just saw."

"Yes, it was rather good." Stirling rose, his broad shoulders filling out his jacket perfectly. "I would offer going to have a nightcap somewhere, but I fear you would turn me down."

"You'd be right." It was best that she went immediately home and regrouped. Right now, she was at risk of turning into a puddle at his feet.

"That's a shame. But we really will need to get past that. No one will believe we're together if you won't let me wine and dine you."

"Is that what you're trying to do?"

The corner of his mouth twitched. "Not very well, if you have to ask." He offered her his hand.

The man had the insane knack of driving her crazy, but also making her feel like a fairytale princess. Accepting his hand, she stood, slightly staggering on her high heels as she realized one foot had fallen asleep. Strong arms gathered her close, supporting her as she found herself cocooned in warmth and sandalwood.

Mortified, she pushed away from his broad chest. "I'm so sorry. I can't believe I just did that."

"I'm not complaining." Stirling smirked at her. "But if you want me to hold you, all you have to do is ask."

"I don't want you to hold me," she ground out. *Liar.*

"Well, since it appears you're in no condition to get yourself home, I insist on driving you."

Cassie's spine snapped straight. I got here under my own steam, and I can get home the same way."

"I wasn't asking, I was telling you." He enunciated each word as if he was speaking to a willful child.

She glared at him. "And I don't need to listen to you."

"Excuse me, is everything all right in here?" An usher pushed back the curtain, securing it.

"Everything is fine, my good man," Stirling assured him, raising a brow at her.

"Just peachy," she said sarcastically.

"In fact, I was just about to drive the young lady home." He offered her a sudden arresting smile. "Isn't that right?"

She wondered if he'd still be smiling if she punched him in the stomach. The thought brought a grin to her own face, one that broadened Stirling's. Knowing he had no idea what had amused her filled Cassie with immense satisfaction. "That's right." *Let the man continue to live dangerously.*

Later after a silent ride home in an insanely expensive car, Cassie looked at her reflection in the mirror. The woman in the flannel cowhide pajamas brushing her teeth didn't look like she'd been on a date with a billionaire. The golden bracelet peeked out from under her sleeve, making her think about Stirling. *Why did he have to ruin what had been an enjoyable evening by becoming a bossy jerk?* Rinsing her mouth, she put her toothbrush back into its holder and made her way to the little dining table that doubled as her desk in the studio apartment. Switching on her laptop, she opened a file and began typing. The one thing that made it all worthwhile was the fact research was coming along nicely.

CHAPTER 5

"I'm sorry, Mr Saint-Claire is in a meeting." The young girl was stunning and quite clearly not impressed with what she saw in front of her.

Cassie adjusted her glasses. Stirling had called that morning and gone over their plan. It seemed like her boyfriend—*pretend boyfriend*—was quite the drama llama when he wanted to be. "I don't think you know who I am, but Mr Saint-Claire will be quite annoyed if you don't let him know I'm here."

"I don't know who you are, and if you think I'm scared by an empty threat like that, then you don't know the actresses and actors I've had to deal with, each and every one threatening me with dire consequences if I don't give them access to Mr Saint-Claire. So, who are you that you think he will drop everything and come out?"

Cassie actually had to give it to the girl, she had balls. In fact, she liked the spunk about her. She pressed her lips together as she brought her hand up to rest lightly on the cold, smooth surface of the reception counter. "I'm his girlfriend."

The receptionist let out a bark of laughter. "Of course you are. I didn't come down in the last shower."

"How about you call his assistant, Angie, and ask her?"

The receptionist eyed her with amusement. "You know that, as soon as I hang up from Angie, I'm going to have to call security and get you escorted from the premises, right? You can save both of us a lot of trouble and just leave now."

"I think I'll wait." Cassie peeked down at the emerald eyes that glittered back at her from her wrist. It was pure vanity that she'd chosen to wear the bracelet today, but now it was oddly reassuring, like a secret symbol that she belonged in this world she was trying to gain access to.

"Suit yourself." The girl picked up the phone and pressed a button. "Angie, have I got one for you. There's a lady here who claims she's Mr Saint-Claire's girlfriend." Her brows twitched downwards. "I'll ask her." She moved the mouthpiece away from her lips. "What's your name."

"Cassie Pearson." She smiled sweetly at her.

"She says her name is Cassie Pearson." The receptionist's gaze slid away as she listened to what was being said to her on the other end. "I see. Yes." Glumly, she hung up the phone. "If you would like a seat, Angie will be out shortly. Can I get you anything to drink while you wait?"

"I thought the next call was to security." Cassie couldn't resist teasing.

"It appears that won't be happening today." The disappointment in the girl's voice almost released the giggle Cassie was doing her best to suppress.

"Miss Pearson." Another attractive blonde appeared, this one with a commanding authoritative air to her. "I'm Angie, Mr Saint-Claire's assistant. I hope you didn't have to wait too long." Angie held her hand out to Cassie, giving a sideways disapproving glare to the luckless receptionist.

"No, I found the wait informative. It has relieved my mind to no end that Stirling is so well protected." The receptionist blushed as she pretended to type something on her computer.

"Excellent. If you would like to come with me." Angie turned to the other woman. "Cancel all of Stirling's appointments for the rest of the day." She smiled knowingly toward Cassie. "He will now be otherwise engaged."

"Cassie," Stirling appeared, his arms encircling her, one hand in the small of her back. "I've missed you, sweetheart." She felt an unwelcomed surge of excitement at his nearness, her heart pounding as he lowered his head, gently rubbing his nose against hers before laying the gentlest of kisses on her lips. It was all Cassie could do not to collapse at his feet. "Angie, I've left the meeting early. Angus is just going to drone on about how the figures support what he's saying. You know what he's like. Could you take care of it for me? I'm going to take this gorgeous lady on a shopping trip."

The receptionist's mouth had dropped open as she stared at the affectionate display taking place in front of her. "Of course," Angie said, smiling approvingly at Cassie. "Make sure he spends big. He can afford it." It dawned on Cassie that Angie might just be the one who had done the research on her.

"The black Amex is going to get a workout today," Stirling amicably agreed. "Now, if you'll excuse us." Guiding Cassie forward with the lightest pressure on the small of her back, he ushered her into a lift. The last thing Cassie saw as the lift door closed was the receptionist's gobsmacked face. "I think that went well, don't you?"

"I think your poor receptionist is having some sort of crisis." Cassie almost felt sorry for her.

"Alice is fine. In fact, she's key to it all. I believe that she feeds things to the press and entertainment sites. If it's front-page news within the hour, I'll know it's true."

"Why do you keep her if you think she's leaking information?" It didn't seem like smart business to her.

"Because I only let her know what I want to be known. She's actually garnered great publicity for various projects since she started working here."

"Is everything a game to you?" Was she a game to him?

"Not everything. I take my business extremely seriously. But there's a secret to not getting burnt out. I actually learned it from my friend, Freddy, who is the most relaxed person I've ever met—except for when it comes to his sister." Stirling waved the thought aside. "You'll understand about Freddy when you meet him tonight. Anyway, the trick is to have fun when you can."

"I'm meeting your friend tonight?" she repeated stupidly. It was news to her.

"Not just him. A few others and their wives as well." He looked her over. "We should probably make sure you have something to wear."

"I have clothes." She stared at him coldly.

"I have a black Amex."

Live the billionaire life. "So, something suitable, you said."

SHOPPING WITH CASSIE had been more fun than Stirling had anticipated. It said a lot for his lifestyle that it wasn't the first time he'd taken a woman shopping. A girl demanding what she wanted to try on, giving him flirtatious eyes as if to secure the purchase. Usually, it was quite simply tiring playing the game. Cassie, on the other hand… Stirling grinned to himself at the memory. She'd strolled into the store on his arm like they were taking a walk in the park. A pleasant smile on her face as she graciously acknowledged the fawning staff. Judging from the way her eyes never quite softened, he'd say the salesgirls' behaviors had changed significantly since she was last there.

Money had a way of making that happen. Except for Cassie. She didn't seem to change. Not since he'd first seen her a couple of nights ago in her red dress. Her expressions always danced across her face, never trying to hide what she was feeling. And she seemed to genuinely live in the moment, absorbing it all, fascinated by the swirling show of life around her. He really should read her books. Maybe they were a snapshot into how she thought.

"This looks a bit fancy." Cassie peered through the window of his town car as it began to pull up to the front steps of the building.

The long black evening dress she wore with a fitted white halter-neck bodice was stunning, her blonde hair piled up on top of her head. Long diamond earrings dangled from each lobe, swinging with every graceful movement. Around the wrist that clutched her evening bag, the emerald eyes of her bracelet glinted back at him. She was an arresting sight, but one that Stirling wished was draped in crimson.

"The British Museum is hosting a fundraiser for local underprivileged children to be better supported at school. My friend, Landon, is actually one of the keynote speakers tonight," he explained.

The car pulled to a stop, the driver quickly opening the door for Stirling to exit. Straightening his jacket, he reached in to help Cassie. His skin tingled when her fingers brushed his. Slightly shaken at his reaction, he looked around as he led her through the distinguished entry. The gray stone columns rose high into the night sky, lit up by downlights, the pediment above showing the creation of man. The large marble-floored foyer gleamed in the lights, reflecting the people who walked upon it.

Stirling sucked in a deep breath, the beauty of the museum hitting him as if for the first time as he recalled Cassie's earlier words. "Yes, it is rather fancy, isn't it?"

"Who's a little fancy?" an American voice asked.

Stirling grinned as he pulled Chora, his best friend's wife, into an embrace, kissing her cheek. "You, of course."

"Smooth." The woman laughed. "Hi, I'm Chora." She extended her hand warmly. "And this"—she pulled a dark-haired woman in closer to them—"is Murphy."

"Hi, I'm Cassie." She flicked him a questioning glance.

"Chora, Murphy, this is my girlfriend, Cassie." Stirling wished he could have captured the stunned look that froze the women's faces. A chuckle escaped him. "Come on now, it can't be that shocking."

"Stirling Saint-Claire, the most outspokenly single bachelor in London except for Freddy—I love him, but he's really a lost cause—has a girlfriend?" Chora gave him a punch in the arm. "Of course it's shocking." She narrowed her eyes at him. "You better not be lying to a pregnant lady." Chora turned to Murphy. "Does he look like he's lying to you?"

Cassie giggled beside him. It had an infectious quality, one he was powerless to resist. He threw his hands up in the air. "Cassie, come to the defense of my honor."

"I don't think he'd lie to a pregnant lady, but I haven't known him that long."

Stirling stared at her in mock horror, enjoying the banter as much as she did. "That's how you defend my honor?"

Cassie shrugged, grinning mischievously up at him. "Well, I don't want to mislead a pregnant lady."

"You know, I already bloody like her," Murphy said in a broad Australian accent. "Plus, we need to even up the numbers for the girl side." She winked at Cassie before looking Chora up and down. "And since you won't tell me what you're having, I can't count on your baby doing it."

It was strange to think that growing inside Chora was the first of the next generation for the friends. Most days he didn't adult enough to even contemplate such a responsibility. Business was one thing, children were quite another. "I'm amazed you and Landon have escaped the clutches of the grandparents."

"We didn't completely escape the grandparents. We're off to see them tomorrow for a few days. They've been disgustingly happy since we told them."

Stirling snorted. "I can imagine. Where is Landon, by the way?" He took some Champagne from the tray of a waiting attendant, handing a glass to each of the ladies except for Chora. "Would you be able to bring something non-alcoholic for the mother-to-be?" he requested.

"Yes, sir. Is there something you'd like in particular?" the man asked solicitously.

"If you have any ginger ale, that would be lovely." Chora turned to the other ladies. "I never used to like it, but since I got pregnant, it's all I want. But it does mean I have to go to the bathroom all the time."

"Chora, dear, I'm not sure I need to hear this," Stirling protested.

An impish grin appeared on her face. "Oh, are you still standing there? I thought you'd left so Murphy and I could get to know Cassie better."

"Well, I would have left you to it, except you haven't told me where Landon is," he pointed out. There was a flush of high color to Cassie's cheek. She seemed to be finding the exchange rather amusing. "But now that I consider it, I don't think I want to leave Cassie alone in your clutches. You might corrupt her."

Murphy gave a hearty laugh. "If she really is your girlfriend, I bloody well doubt there's anything we could say that would shock her."

Chora gave a slow shake of her head as she sighed. "So mean to a pregnant lady. Landon is with Freddy over near the dinosaur skeleton." She accepted the glass from the returned waiter. "But I know how you boys are when you get together." Chora winked at Cassie. "It's much more fun with the girls." She eyeballed Stirling. "And I promise to take good care of her and not give away all of your secrets. How about that?"

Cassie reached out, her fingers warm where they stroked his arm. Stirling momentarily forgot what he was going to say, caught up in the sensation. "Stirling, it's okay. I'll be fine here with Chora and Murphy. I'm sure we'll have lot to talk about."

"That's what I'm worried about," he muttered. He pressed a kiss to her cheek, enjoying the delightful way she blushed as the other women gave each other meaningful glances. "As long as you will be all right. I promise I won't be too long."

"I'll be fine." She made a shooing motion. "Go find your friends."

As Stirling went in search of Landon and Freddy, he found that he liked the idea of Cassie getting on with Chora and Murphy more than he would have expected. Now, to go get royally roasted by his friends about having a girlfriend.

THIS CINDERELLA, *having gone to her first ball, never wanted to leave.* Cassie rubbed at her aching cheeks, looking over the notes she'd written down. *In a building that borrowed the decadence of the Greeks and Romans, culture gleaming from every corner. Richly dressed elegant ladies, squired by their handsome husbands. Laughter and friendship amongst diamonds, fossils and*

Champagne. It wasn't at all what Cassie had expected a society event to be like. Heck, she hadn't expected to like his friends as much as she had. And the way they'd welcomed her—she felt horrible lying to them, but she'd simply followed Stirling's lead. *I wonder where he'll lead me next.*

35

"**How** is my favorite girlfriend feeling this morning?" Stirling's rich baritone flowed warmly through the phone.

"I wasn't aware that you had more than one. Pretend ones, at least," Cassie quickly added. Self-consciously, she glanced down at the oversized T-shirt, Mickey Mouse front and center on it. This probably wasn't the usual type of nightwear his girlfriends wore. Running her tongue over her fuzzy teeth, she smoothed her hair down. "Isn't it a bit early to be calling?"

"I like to feel we have the sort of pretend relationship that means we are there for each other, night or day." Was it her imagination or was there almost a wistful quality to his words? Stirling didn't exactly seem like the type. "Was I interrupting something?"

"Only my sleep. What time is it anyway?" Cassie fumbled around, trying to locate her phone. *Idiot.* She sighed noisily, rolling her eyes at her own stupidity.

"It's after eight in the morning. I take it you're not much of an early riser?" Stirling teased her.

"Well, I can be. Sometimes. When I get the words flowing, I try to keep writing until they stop and that can be quite late into the night."

"Did you write last night after I dropped you home?" Curiosity tinged his voice.

"I didn't work on a story, just notes and thoughts." *A lot of thoughts centering on one Englishman in particular.*

"Well, it's a good thing I let you sleep in. There's a car that will be coming to collect you at twelve. You'll need to pack a bag for a few days. I think it's time we had some fun before we need to fly to LA for my work."

"Hang on, where are we going?" She searched her mind, vaguely remembering him mentioning some sort of itinerary. "What do I pack?"

"It's time I introduce you to the French Riviera. Pack what you think will be suitable. Whatever you don't bring, I'll buy you once we're there."

Cassie swallowed. So casually said. *The French Riviera,* just casually tossed out like it was a trip to Walmart. "I guess I should get packing."

"Oh, and Cassie?"

"Yes?"

"Wear the red dress."

Cassie's knees turned to jelly at the command. "And if I don't?"

"One way or another, it's going to happen, Little Red." He purred the warning to her.

Sure, he was being high-handed, but dang if it didn't get her heart beating faster. "I'm not sure I like you telling me what to do."

"I suggest you get used to it. Be ready at twelve." And the line went dead.

Cassie stared at her phone for a moment longer. It appeared like this billionaire liked to get what he wanted.

Opening her wardrobe, she nibbled on her lip as she stared at the dress in question. *I wonder what he'll do if I don't? Would the Big Bad Wolf come out to play?*

STIRLING'S MOUTH puckered in displeasure. She was most definitely not wearing the red dress. Amusement rippled through him that he tried to keep from his expression. Little Red was showing that she had claws. There was something incredibly attractive about her giving zero concerns about what he wanted, at least for now. He was going to change her mind about doing what he told her to do, or at least try, and wasn't that half the fun?

Cassie stared around at the interior of his private jet. Everything was done in dark mahogany and black leather with gold accents. It gave a distinctly masculine vibe, like a wolf's den. She met his eye and raised her chin defiantly. "Hello, Stirling. Nice plane."

He raised a lazy brow at her, daring her to hold his gaze. Stirling was pleased when her eyes wavered ever so slightly before snapping back to him. "I see you aren't wearing your red dress."

"I might be new to this whole live-like-a-billionaire caper, but somehow it felt like I was going to be a little over-dressed." Her casual tone seemed a little overdone. Clearly she wasn't as unaffected as she was trying to make out.

His gaze swept over her, taking in the tie-dyed baggy sweats that she was wearing in place of the requested garment. "And this is what you deemed a more suitable choice?" Stirling offered her a sudden arresting grin. "I don't think anyone has ever worn them on this plane before."

That stubborn little chin jutted out, if possible, even further. "Well, now you know. I'm a trendsetter."

An adorable trendsetter. "That you are. Now, if you'd like to take your seat, we can get cleared to take off."

Cassie scrunched up her face before poking her tongue out at him. "Now that's out of the way, I guess I can." Taking the seat next to him, she clicked her seatbelt into place. "This is my first time on a private plane—I'm sorry, jet. Are they all as nice as this?"

"Without sounding conceited, there are possibly five planes that would be considered more luxurious than the one you currently have your sweatpants clad self in." She looked rather comfortable in her clothing choice. Sure, it wasn't the red dress, and he hadn't given up on seeing her in it again, but it made the two of them sitting together feel homely, familiar. It had been a long time since Stirling had had that feeling with anyone who wasn't part of his close friendship circle. It was nice.

"What's the inflight entertainment like?"

"You're looking at it."

"Well, that's a little disappointing." Cassie giggled. It was infectious, and Stirling found himself grinning in response. "I'd thought with how luxurious"—she stressed the word—"this plane is, that it would come better equipped."

"Ouch." He held a hand to his heart. "I'll have you know that no one has ever complained about my equipment before."

Cassie flipped open a notebook. "No excuses for not getting some work done, I guess. How long is the flight anyway?"

"A little over two hours. What are you working on?" He tried to get a look at the words scrawled across the page, but she quickly closed it.

"Just notes."

"What sort of notes?"

"All sorts. It might be little impressions of places, or an

expression, maybe a smell, a way a person has of speaking. I put it all in here."

Most writers Stirling had met all had their own process. He wondered what Cassie's was. "What comes first, the idea for a story or the characters?"

She nibbled her pen as she thought. "Sometimes it will be a vague idea for a story, other times characters won't leave me alone until I give them a story of their own."

He laughed. "They won't leave you alone?"

A small smile enchanted her lips. "Oh, yes. Some are quite persistent, always giving me little snippets that need to be used."

"Am I giving you lots of little snippets to be used?"

Stains of scarlet appeared on her cheeks. "That's a little arrogant don't you think? Not you personally as much as what you've shown me."

Interesting. I think the lady protests too much. "Well, if you ever need me to give you some material for your next character…" He left it hanging.

Cassie stiffened and turned in her seat to look out her window. "I think I'll be fine. The research you're helping me with for how billionaires live is quite enough."

Very interesting indeed.

CASSIE TRIED, she really did, to not stare around like some sort of country hick as Stirling led her into the villa. "Is that a dinosaur skeleton?" she exclaimed, pointing to the corner of the living area they had just entered.

Stirling tugged at his ear, smiling at the woman that approached them. "I believe it's a full-sized replica of a dinosaur fossil, is that correct, Brielle?"

"That is correct, Monsieur Saint-Claire." The woman

smiled politely at Cassie. "I am Brielle, and I am your hostess for your stay in this villa. Would you like me to show you around?"

"That's not necessary." Stirling waved her suggestion away. "I've stayed here enough to know the lay of the land. I think I'm qualified enough to show Cassie around."

"Of course," the woman said in her pleasant French accent. "If there is anything you require, please let me know."

"Can you please tell the chef that we will dine out on the terrace this evening?" Stirling's hand fit intimately into the small of Cassie's back as he ushered her from the room. "I believe my assistant emailed through my request for the meal."

"She did. I'll have it arranged for you." Brielle turned and glided soundlessly from the room.

"You don't own this place?" Cassie asked. It hadn't occurred to her that they would stay in a rented accommodation. Somehow she'd just assumed Stirling owned it.

"No." Stirling gave a little apologetic shrug of his shoulders. "I have properties in LA, London, New York, Mustique and Aspen. But here's something to write down in your notes. Most wealthy people, they borrow other wealthy people's possessions. This house, for instance, belongs to a movie director I know. A superyacht we will be using tomorrow belongs to an oil tycoon."

"Kinda like if you scratch my back, I'll scratch yours?"

"Exactly. Now, since you seem so interested in this villa. Let me tell you a little about it. Just for your research, of course. It has eight bedrooms of which, for this stay, only two will be used. That is, unless you wish to sleep in a different bedroom each night." He gave her a naughty sideways glance.

Cassie wasn't quite sure why she felt the need to blush again. "I think I can manage with just the one bedroom."

He shook his head at her in mock sadness. "You really need to start thinking like a billionaire."

"Or a billionaire's girlfriend."

"At the very least. As well as several living areas, there's also a cinema room, wine cellar, gym, which can double as a dance studio if you wish. Do you think you'll want to get some dance practice in while we are here?"

She giggled. "I have two left feet, so no."

"Maybe with more practice you could fix that, and there's the perfect room at your disposal for it."

"No." She tapped him on the arm. "It's never going to happen."

His gaze deepened, a heat flaring to life. "Never say never." He blinked, and Cassie found herself wondering if she'd imagined it. "There's also the jacuzzi and then the staff. You've met Brielle already, but there's also a full-time chef at your disposal, some gardeners and housekeepers and security."

"Security? Why do we need security?" Alarmed, she froze, looking around, feeling like baddies could jump out from behind the next outlandish sculpture they went by.

"When you are wealthy, security is just a part of life."

"But you don't have any."

"I do, especially at my homes. When I have events that I know the general public will know who I am and where I'll be, I'll always take a bodyguard. It's just being prudent."

Cassie shivered. Suddenly being a billionaire didn't seem so awesome after all. "I guess."

Stirling gave her a little nudge forward, setting her feet into motion toward a glass French door, the white chiffon curtains billowing in the breeze. "All of this is set on just over an acre of manicured garden, but the piece de resistance, as I'm sure you'll agree, is this." He pushed the door open.

In front of her awestruck eyes was an immense infinity

pool that stretched the length of the house, beginning where the sun-drenched terrace ended. Beyond she could see rolling emerald hills that spilled down into the glistening coastline and the entire azure bay of Cannes. It hit her how fortunate she was to see a view that only a very exclusive group had the privilege of seeing. "It's amazing."

"Is that the best you've got, miss hotshot author?"

"Okay, how about stupendous, enthralling, overwhelming, flabbergasting, amazeballs."

Stirling let out a snort. "I can't decide out of flabbergasting or amazeballs, which are my favorites."

"There's no need to pick one, just use them as you see fit. It's my gift to you. Speaking of which, if you could show me to my room, I need to change."

His eyes lit up. "Into your red dress?"

"No." She rolled her eyes. "I'm getting hot in my sweats. I want to change into something a little more summery."

"Like a bikini?"

"I wasn't planning on it, no."

"Well, if you change into a bikini, we can test out the pool."

Cassie narrowed her eyes at him. "I imagine you've tested the pool out on your previous visits." Jealousy jagged at her at the thought of who else he might have tested it with. *Whoa, calm down, girl. Remember, this is all pretend.*

"True. How about this." He knelt beside the pool. "I can personally vouch for the quality of this pool and its stupendous views and if you try it, I think you'll find it completely amazeballs." He splashed her with a handful of water.

"How can a girl say no to an invitation like that?"

"That was the plan. Otherwise I was just going to throw you over my shoulder and jump in with you."

Cassie stared at his expensive outfit. *This man had more money than sense.* "It would ruin your clothes."

"But you're not worried about yours?" He quirked a brow at her. "Does that mean I should just throw you in, instead?"

"No." She hastily backed through the French doors. "It'll take more than some pool water to ruin my sweats. They're indestructible. Still, doesn't mean I want to risk it."

Stirling prowled in after her. There was something primal to the way he stalked her, and Cassie found herself growing warm. *Maybe the pool wasn't such a bad idea after all.* "Well, in that case, I suggest you go get changed."

"But you haven't shown me my room yet," she protested, still backing away.

"Go back to the dinosaur and turn left. The next door down the hall is yours. But if you take too long"—he gave her a heated look—"I can't promise the dry condition of your sweats."

With a squeal, Cassie took off. This wasn't how she'd expected to act in a villa in Cannes. Somehow it was even better.

EVERY YEAR, Stirling came to Cannes, usually for the film festival. The town turning into a seething nest of celebrity, the paparazzi on every corner trying to capture the perfect angle, stars walking the red carpet after arriving via boats— there was a hunger to it all. Now seated on the terrace, he watched as the lights of other villas and the town twinkled in the night, the boats on the harbor gently swaying with the rhythm of the sea. He rubbed at his still damp hair, gazing at Cassie at the other end of the table over the rim of his wine- glass. They'd left it till the very last minute to get out of the pool, the aroma of the meal being placed on the table finally enough to drive them from the water. He'd hastily thrown on a shirt, leaving it open at the front, Cassie covering herself with a kaftan, her hair pulled back into a wet messy bun on top of her head. The woman simply didn't care that she wasn't groomed to within an inch of her life. She was even more glorious because of it.

"You mentioned that you—" She swallowed a mouthful of wine quickly. *Was she nervous?* "I mean, *we* have to go to LA for work." She picked another piece of seafood from her plate and delicately placed it in her mouth, slowly chewing as if to savor every morsel of it. Stirling was riveted.

"I take it you like the bouillabaisse?" Stirling had never been jealous of food before. *Turns out there was a first time for everything.* "Yes, we have a project that is going into production." He hoped it wasn't as big a headache as the last one.

"What does it actually involve? I'm never quite sure when I see it in the credits."

He took a sip of his wine, pondering how to condense what he did into a simple explanation. "Well, some of the time, someone can be listed in the credits as a producer, but not do anything other than provide funding or in exchange for rights."

Cassie nodded sagely, her eyes owlish. Maybe it was time to stop filling up her wineglass. He'd no idea she was such a lightweight. It was actually rather endearing given the culture of hard-drinking, hard-partying celebrities he normally found himself surrounded by. "Somehow I don't think that's the kind of producer you are."

Stirling's smile broadened in approval. "You're right, I'm not. I sit at the top of the pyramid, making all the decision that goes toward getting a film made. The responsibility for a project being successful also ends with me. My team find and launch a project, arrange financing, hire writers, a director, key members of the creative team, and even have a say on casting. Basically, I oversee all elements of pre-production, production and post-production right up to release."

"Whoa, that's a lot of responsibility." She pushed her bowl away from her and, with a look of concentration on her face, dabbed at her mouth with her napkin. *Yes, definitely time to cut her off.* "But I think you like telling people what to do, and even more when they do what they're told."

The way she looked at him made him feel primal. "You could say that," he said in a low growl. *Settle down, old chap.* Taking a firmer grip on his wineglass than was wise given the fragile nature of the object, he drained it. *Time to get onto safer topics.* "Where are you from originally?"

Cassie straightened herself with dignity, at odds with her slow blinking expression. "Boise, Idaho."

Hell, she was adorable. Stirling laughed gently, rubbing his wrist with his thumb. "A romance writer from Idaho in the French Riviera with a British boyfriend headed back to LA. There's a book in that."

"I think there's a book in you. Not the one I thought I was going to write, maybe not even this one. Maybe I'll give you a whole series. About a big bad wolf." Her head began to droop slowly as her words trailed off.

"Okay, Little Red, time you stop drinking and get to bed."

She gave a hiccupping giggle. "You're a poet."

Stirling put a firm arm under her shoulder and pulled her to her feet. He tightened his grip on her as she oozed into him. "I think I remember I told you I had a lot of skills."

"You were right."

Stirling gently but firmly led his drunk Little Red toward her room, making a mental note to only ever give her two glasses of wine, or at least make sure they were more spaced apart. "Okay, Cassie, we're here. Do I need to call Brielle to help you?"

"I don't think Brielle can help me," she slurred slightly.

"Why? I assure you, she's highly competent in her role."

Cassie leaned in closer. He could smell the wine on her breath. "Because I want you to kiss me."

Desire slammed into him, followed by the realization that nothing was going to happen, not like this. "I think this might be a discussion for another day."

She pouted, giving a huffy little sigh. "Not even a good-night kiss?"

Slowly, he closed the distance between them until he gave her lips the merest brush with his own. The moment barely lasted an instant before he pulled back, knowing his restraint would only last so much. "Goodnight, Cassie."

She stared at him with huge eyes, gently touching where his lips had been moments earlier. "Goodnight, Stirling." With one last glance, she stepped back through the doorway, closing it behind her. Standing there in the now empty hallway, Stirling could only mutter that sometimes being a gentleman wasn't all it was cracked up to be before stalking away in search of a cold shower.

MANY TALENTS, good kisser, I wish—

The pen slipped from Cassie's slack hand, a soft snore sounding.

CHAPTER 7

Cassie swallowed, her mouth feeling decidedly tacky. It hit her that she'd been drinking wine. And not just any wine, but her archnemesis in alcoholic form—her kryptonite—red wine. She stared up at the ceiling, a rolling nausea lashing her insides. *Please don't let me have made too big a fool of myself last night.* She quickly began to play over the evening's events. The pool had been amazing, leaning on the edge of it looking down over the sprawling vista below. Her billionaire was definitely getting an infinity pool in her book. So far Cassie didn't see any reason for concern. She hadn't had any wine at that stage—it had come when they'd emerged dripping from the pool, the pull of a sumptuous meal too great to ignore any longer. That's when she'd weakened, accepting the glass from Brielle when she'd inquired if everything was to their liking.

The meal had been everything the mouthwatering aromas had promised and then some, and the conversation flowed freely. She distinctly remembered feeling relaxed and content in Stirling's company until the wine had made her begin to feel drowsy and she'd decided to head to bed. Stirling, ever the gentleman, had escorted her back to her room. And then it slammed into her with the force of a thunderbolt, the memory burning with a sting of embarrassment. She touched her lips with shaking fingers as if she could still feel the tingle of his touch. She'd asked him to kiss her! Cassie pulled the covers over her head. Was it possible for her to spend the rest of her time in Cannes hiding under the sheets?

"Good morning, Cassie. I trust you slept well."

If Cassie could make herself look Stirling in the eyes, she knew she would see the amusement that filled the simple greeting staring back at her. "It was satisfactory, thank you," she muttered, sitting down at the table.

Brielle materialized before Cassie's bum had even made contact with the chair. "It's a beautiful morning." Her overly white teeth beamed from her smile. "What would you like for breakfast?"

"Um, what did Stirling have?" Cassie wasn't sure how to respond. She'd never had someone ask her what she wanted. Usually she just picked something off the menu at the local diner.

"I haven't had anything except for two cups of coffee while I waited for you to appear."

Guilt mixed with the oily feeling in her belly, and she peeked up to see him regarding her with open amusement, quickly chasing her earlier emotion away. "I'm sorry. I didn't know that breakfast was at a set time."

"It isn't. If it was, I'd have made sure you were here for it." There was that note of command again. Her poor belly fluttered in response. "Would you like me to order for you as well?"

"I'll just have what you have." Cassie picked up the glass of water in front of her and drained it, Brielle quickly refilling it.

"Excellent. Brielle, we will both have an acai bowl." The hostess gave a smooth nod before gliding from the room. Stirling gave Cassie an appraising look. "How are you feeling this morning?"

"Fine. Is there a reason I shouldn't be?" The thought of asking him to kiss her last night flashed mortifyingly into her brain.

"I didn't realize that you had such a weak head for wine. It was rather … cute."

Cassie's head snapped up to glare at him with narrowed eyes. "Cute? And it isn't all wine, just red wine."

He chuckled, the rich sound rolling through the room. "Ironic. Little Red can't drink red—at least without it going to her head."

"Argh." She scrunched up her face. "Don't start."

"You seemed to like it last night." He smirked at her. "Enough to want to kiss me."

"And that's all the more reason why I'm not drinking it again when I'm around you."

"A shame, really." There was a heat to the way he looked at her when he said it. Did he want her to ask him to kiss her again? "Since you seem to be feeling quite well this morning, when we finish breakfast, we will be heading out on a little excursion."

Getting out of the villa into some fresh air might be just what the doctor ordered. "Oh, anywhere in particular?"

"Yes, as a matter of fact." He smiled up at Brielle as she placed a bowl in front of him. "Thank you."

The hostess placed the other bowl in front of Cassie. It was filled with a purple puree, topped with sliced fruit and granola. Cassie picked up her spoon and poked at the contents. "And are you going to tell me?"

Stirling popped a blueberry into his mouth. "I don't think I will. But you should pack a bikini."

Cassie brought her spoon dubiously closer to her mouth. *If I didn't know better, it's just an excuse to see me in a swimsuit again.* Curiosity tugged at her. *I will, just to find out where we're going.*

"THAT'S A REALLY BIG BOAT." Cassie stood with her beach bag hanging slack by her side as she stared up at the behemoth in front of her.

"It's actually a yacht." Stirling took her bag from her and gently ushered her toward the gangway.

"I've seen yachts before," she protested, holding the handrail as she stepped gingerly onto the gently swaying platform. "You know, with a sail. This doesn't look anything like one."

"Welcome aboard, Mr Saint-Claire, and if I might presume to answer the young lady's question?" a smartly dressed man said. Cassie assumed he was the captain. Who knew? Clearly not her since she didn't even know the difference between a boat and a yacht.

"Please do, Captain Morgan." Stirling set her bag down on the deck.

"There's no official definition for what is or isn't a yacht. However, it is applied to vessels such as this, which is a luxurious pleasure vessel that is professionally crewed." The captain looked proudly about him. "And given her size, she's referred to as a superyacht."

"Does that clear things up for you?" Stirling asked solicitously. She nodded dumbly. Cassie had never seen anything like this, and her brain was having a hard time processing. She'd been on a cruise ship once which had been like a floating city, but that had been filled with people. This immense floating structure simply had the crew, Stirling and herself onboard. "Captain, Cassie here is doing some research for a book. Would you be able to tell her a little about The Bonnita?"

"I'd be happy to." Cassie got the impression that the boat —*excuse me, yacht, excuse me, superyacht*—was very much the man's baby. "The Bonnita is almost one hundred and forty-six yards long, has a top speed of twenty-five knots and comfortably cruises at fifteen knots. She can accommodate up to twenty-four guests in twelve cabins comprising of one VIP stateroom, seven double cabins and three twin cabins. She is also capable of carrying up to sixty-two crew in thirty crew cabins."

Cassie gave an amazed whistle. "That's a lot of people."

Captain Morgan smiled proudly. "It is, and it guarantees that we can offer maximum luxury for our guests."

"Tell her about the features The Bonnita offers." Stirling gave her a little nudge. "You might want to get your notebook out for this one."

"She comes equipped with what you would usually expect. WiFi connection, deck jacuzzi, stabilizers, and two helipads."

"Of course," Cassie muttered. "Is it even a superyacht if it doesn't have those?"

"Not in this day and age," Captain Morgan agreed. "The Bonnita also offers a helicopter hangar, an exhaustive list of toys, an internal seawater swimming pool as well as the swimming pool you can see on the sundeck that offers a wet bar, pizza oven and teppanyaki grill." He paused to draw breath. "The submarine hangar, cinema, indoor climbing wall, underwater viewing room, dedicated children's playroom, which I don't expect will be of much use this trip." There was a mischievous sparkle in his eye as he grinned at the two of them. "Maybe next time."

Cassie's cheeks burned at his comment. "This must be one of the most expensive superyachts there is."

Captain Morgan coughed uncomfortably. "I love The Bonnita, but she's actually surpassed by The History Supreme."

"What is it made of? Gold?" Cassie laughed at her own joke.

Stirling's mouth twisted into a wry smile. "Actually, it is. Over twenty-two thousand pounds of solid gold and platinum. It's everywhere—even the anchor. I guess for $4.8 billion dollars it would want to be."

"It's a crazy yacht," Captain Morgan agreed. "The master stateroom even has a meteorite rock wall and a liquor bottle that has an eighteen and a half carat diamond set into it. I could talk shop all day, but if you're happy, I'd like to depart."

Stirling gave Cassie a grin like he couldn't wait to show her her surprise. "Unless Cassie has any more questions, I think that's a great idea. Cassie?"

Her mind still reeling at the information overload, she blinked when she found herself on the receiving end of both men's looks. "Oh? Yeah, sure, that sounds good." Following in Stirling's wake, Cassie realized that she was so far out of her depths it wasn't funny. Her imagination was good, but it didn't compare to what billionaires considered normal.

WHEN STIRLING HAD DECIDED to plan the itinerary for the outing, he'd gravitated to places he enjoyed. He reasoned that it was only natural that if he liked them, she should too. He tried not to think that he was showing them to her because he wanted her to feel how special they were the way he felt about them. Going to the Iles de Lerins was a prime example. He could justify it because it was the home to the legendary Man in the Iron Mask, something a writer would find fascinating. It could be the fact there were historical churches and remains of forts all set in a stunning natural setting.

Now, after seeing how the night before had impacted Cassie, there was a certain irony that the real reason he'd selected this island for a stopover was so that she would have the opportunity to taste the wine from the vineyards of the Ile Saint-Honorat, made by the legendary monks of the Lerins Abbey.

"Vines have been cultivated on this island since the Middle Ages," the monk leading them through the monastery said in a friendly, slightly rusty voice. Stirling wondered if the only time he spoke was to lead visitors around the grounds. There was a sense of peace here. The monks he had seen all appeared to come from diverse backgrounds, and yet the serenity was inescapable.

"Then you must know a thing or two about winemaking," Cassie said brightly.

"Which is good, since she knows a thing or two about red wine," Stirling added teasingly.

"Hush," she murmured, giving him a warning look. "What varieties do you grow here?"

"Pinot noir, chardonnay, syrah and mourvedre," the monk replied.

"You're in luck, Cassie, they do a red." He wasn't sure why he enjoyed teasing her. All he knew was that he couldn't stop. It might be the way she chewed the inside of her lip as she pretended to ignore him, or the narrowing of her eyes as she fired warning glances his way all while the color on her cheeks bloomed. It was addictive.

Ignoring the by-play around him, the monk continued his

tour. "Every stage is carried out by hand, and we produce Saint Salonius, Saint Lambert, Saint Cesaire, Saint Sauveur, Saint Cyprien, Saint Honorat and Saint Pierre. The last is generally considered to be one of the best and finest French wines."

"That's a lot of saints," Stirling whispered to Cassie.

"Behave," she whispered back warningly.

Stirling cleared his throat. "Do you happen to have any of the Saint Pierre available?"

"Yes."

"Excellent, we'll take a couple of bottles for later. Now, Cassie, do you have any other questions for the nice monk?" The day wasn't over yet, and Stirling still had other plans.

"I do, actually." *Of course she did. She wanted to know everything. If she ever gave up on her writing career, she could have a red hot go at game shows.* "What is it like living here? It seems so peaceful, but what do you do in your daily life?"

The monk gave her the first genuine smile Stirling had seen cross his face since they'd been placed in his care. It took years off him, which wasn't saying much. "We live a communal life here. It's structured by prayer, work, study and hospitality, and I'd never felt such belonging and enlightenment before I entered these walls. I was called to this life later than others and I will spend the rest of it in service of our Lord."

Stirling was still mulling his words over when they pulled up just outside the secluded cove. The way the man had looked as he'd stared into space, his features composed into soft lines, and the utter conviction in his voice. It had caused the hairs on Stirling's arms to stand up. He wasn't sure he'd ever felt that level of conviction in his life, and he'd dealt with fame-hungry starlets.

Cassie ambled over to him, a strawberry in hand. "I see the crew have been feeding you," he noted dryly.

"Lunch will be ready shortly." She took another bite, the juices painting her lips scarlet. It was an arresting sight. "Apparently I'm to tell you that they are ready when you are."

"Excellent. Did you pack a bikini like I asked?"

"Yes."

"Go get changed, and then we can get started."

"Started on what? Are we going to use the jacuzzi?"

"Even better."

Later as the salt water sprayed in their faces, with her arms around him holding on for dear life as they sped across the turquoise waters, he stared up at the gargantuan yacht and realized he'd much rather be down here with Cassie than up there with a hundred models. It was a confronting thought, and one that jolted him from the moment. His hands clenched on the handlebars of the watercraft, his arms jerking. With a startled cry, Cassie launched from behind him, tumbling ungainly into the water.

Darn it. He quickly dove into the water after her, reaching her side as she made the surface of the water, coughing and splattering. "What the heck?" She pushed her wet locks off her face as she treaded water. "One minute, we're zipping across the sea, and the next it's only me doing it but with cartwheels."

"Sorry, I lost control and before I knew it, you were already in the drink." There was no way he was going to admit what really happened. He made a show of glancing at his watch. "It's time we stow the jet ski anyway if we want to make it to Saint-Tropez in time for dinner."

Cassie began to breaststroke back toward the watercraft. "You could have just told me that instead of trying to clear out my sinus cavity with a blast of salt water," she grumbled.

"How about I make up for it with a massage?" He swam easily beside her, the jet ski now within grasping distance as he easily pulled himself up from the warm water. Securing himself, he reached back down and lifted Cassie from the sea as easily as plucking a feather from the ground. "It will give you the opportunity to warm up. A nice glass of Champagne, the sun gently toasting your skin as you relax."

She wrapped her wet arms around him again, pulling herself snuggly against him. She obviously wasn't taking any chances of doing more aquatic acrobats, but having her body mold to him was making his brain suggest all kind of exciting things to him. "Is there a masseur onboard?"

Stirling put the toggle that was fastened securely around his wrist back into the jet ski. "You're looking at him." Whatever she had to say was lost in the revving of the engine as he gunned it, eager to get to that sundeck.

THE *THWOP THWOP* of the helicopter blades slicing through the air and holding them in the sky was a steady companion to the gentle sigh-like snores coming from Cassie. *Poor girl was plumb tuckered out from her day.* He pulled the blanket he'd draped over her higher up to her chin, Cassie not stirring at all. On the seat beside her, her notepad lay. For a moment, he considered flipping through its pages. Would he find mentions of himself? Would he like what she thought of him? Feeling like it would be intruding or perhaps that he didn't want to shatter the illusion he had of how she saw him, he settled back.

He could be certain of one thing—she would have pages of observations from their dinner in Saint-Tropez. The restaurant that overlooked the harbor was a prime location for people watching, and he'd thought that Cassie's head was about to swivel off as she tried to take it all in at the same time. The table with the models all ordering salads but not eating anything as they consumed Champagne and smoked cigarettes. The older society ladies with their jewels worn like armor against the harsh glare of youth. The elderly men with their young wives. The elderly women with their young husbands. Everywhere was wealth and privilege. *It should be a great insight for her book.* He turned, staring out the window at the lights of the villas clinging to the side of the hills below. It was an insight into his life.

"CASSIE." The merman swam closer. She could just barely make him out through the tangle of her hair gently swaying in the ocean current. He was beautiful, the way the scales on his tail glinted in the rays of light. "Cassie." The merman's voice had an edge of gentle laughter to it. She knew in her bones she would follow that sound anywhere. The water was getting rougher, and she could feel herself getting shaken by it. "Cassie, you need to wake up. We're back at the villa." *Mermen had villas? That didn't sound right.*

Strong arms drew her in close, cradling her to him. *Who knew mermen were so warm? That definitely didn't seem right!* Her eyes snapped open, and she found herself tucked with her head in the hollow of Stirling's chest.

"You're not a merman," she stammered, disoriented, embarrassment burning brightly. "What are you doing? Put me down."

Those arms lowered her gently to the ground, but not before she felt his laughter rumbling through his chest. "Do I even want to know what that means?"

Cassie straightened her clothes. "Clearly, I was dreaming." She marched through the villa doorway. "The last thing I remember is getting into the helicopter, and then I must have fallen asleep."

"You were very cute, Little Red, all tucked in with your blanket." Stirling easily matched her steps.

Reaching the door to her room, she determinedly pushed away her mortification at babbling in her sleep. *About mermen, of all crazy things.* The day he'd given her … heck, the whole time he'd been her boyfriend—*pretend boyfriend*—and what he'd given her hadn't been short of amazing. "Thanks for today. I don't think I could have even begun to imagine people doing what we did today."

He leaned a shoulder against the doorframe, peering at her like he could see her soul. "What was your favorite part?"

"Climbing on an inside climbing wall that was inside a superyacht as we drank Champagne and sailed the French Riviera. That definitely was something."

"Mine was seeing the sun glisten of the baby oil as I gave you a massage. Believe me, *that* was definitely something." His gaze deepened, became more dangerous.

Cassie licked her lips nervously, her heart pounding in her chest. "It's time I go to bed." She found his nearness both disturbing and exciting.

"I was thinking the same thing." Stirling pushed himself lazily off the wall.

She could feel the warmth of his body, her heart going into overtime. "I meant alone." She was dismayed to hear the slight break in her voice.

He quirked a brow as if to say that they both knew she wasn't as committed as she wanted to appear. Stirling leaned forward. Cassie could only stare wide-eyed as he lowered his head to hers and, with the merest brush of his lips, gave her a chaste kiss. "Goodnight, Little Red." His voice was husky, its intimacy sending a delightful shiver down her spine.

She swallowed hard, lifted her chin, and boldly met his eyes. "I don't remember asking you to kiss me tonight."

He gave her a smile that set her pulse racing. "You didn't

have to. I know it's what you wanted." Stirling made no move to step back yet. "Tell me, Little Red, what do you write in your little notebook about me?"

Cassie snapped her mouth shut, stunned at his arrogant bluntness or maybe how close to home it struck. "It's a little egotistical to think I write about you, isn't it?"

Stirling smirked at her, pure male pride. "It's not ego if it's true. In which case, it's confidence, and that"—he reached out and gently stroked her cheek—"is something I have in spades," he purred.

Cassie's legs turned to jelly. She knew without a trace of doubt that, in that moment, she would fall over the abyss to wherever he wanted to take her if he just asked. With a final tender stroke, he turned and walked away. With shaking hands, she fumbled with the door handle and made her way inside, throwing her bag and notepad on the desk.

Torn by conflicting emotions and feeling overly warm, she paced around the room. Turning back to the desk, she pounced on the notepad and added one final note for the day with slashing strokes.

Insufferably arrogant, but I wish he would kiss me like his soul needed me.

Never think about mermen again! Ever!

CHAPTER 8

"I'm actually surprised you remained awake for the entire duration of this helicopter flight," Stirling said lightly. With Cassie sitting opposite him in that red dress—one that had spent entirely too much time teasing his dreams—he'd never felt so awake.

"You let me sleep in today and didn't trek me up and down the entire French Riviera, and you told me to dress up," she replied tartly, but he could see the glimmer of mischief in her eyes. *She enjoys our banter as much as I do.*

"I am still trekking you a fair way. All the way to Monaco today." It might have been so he'd have an excuse to see her dressed up. "And just like that, we're here."

"That was good timing." Cassie peered out the window of the helicopter as it descended onto the helipad.

Stirling knew their car would be waiting just out of sight, ready to whisk them away. "I always have good timing. Or haven't you realized that yet?"

"I'm beginning to realize quite a few things about you," she said, a mysterious smile gracing her lips. *Really?* What else could she have realized about him? His stomach tightened at the flirtatious tone in her voice and, with it, all its implications.

"That you're the perfect person to help me research my book." Cassie unclicked her seatbelt, smiling a hello to the attendant as her door was opened. As he'd known, a car stood waiting. A short walk later and they were both safely ensconced and on to their final destination.

"Have you ever been to the Casino de Monte-Carlo?" It was only a quick drive and he found himself not wanting to spend it in silence. Or was it that he didn't want the flirting to stop?

She gave him a look that quite clearly said he'd have more luck if he'd asked her about the last time she'd seen a yeti. "I haven't even been to Monaco before. But I have read about it. The glitz, the glamor." She sighed longingly, her hand with the panther bracelet on the wrist over her heart. "The stuff a romance writer's dreams are made of." Cassie turned, her nose almost pressed to the glass of the car's window. "Everyone is so over-the-top here. Like, it was full on in Cannes, but this is next level. Every woman we've passed so far has been carrying a designer bag and they're all dressed impeccably. Does anyone just get around wearing normal, comfy clothes?"

"But how would people know they're wealthy?"

"That's a good point." She giggled. "No good being disgustingly rich if no one knows you are."

"Exactly."

The car pulled up, waiting to get to the head of the line. It was now after two pm, and the valets were zipping in and out of an array of Ferraris, Bentleys, Rolls-Royces and everything in between. As the night settled in, the Belle Epoque architecture would be displayed to perfection by the lighting. Somehow nothing was classier than marble and gold.

"I'm not going to lie, I'm going to be incredibly disappointed if I don't meet an international spy tonight."

Seizing the opportunity, he gave her his best man-of-mystery smile. "Will I do?"

Cassie eyed him up and down covetously, taking in his bespoke ebony suit, the custom shoes. He felt rather confident that he would make a superb spy. "In a pinch."

"In a pinch," he spluttered. *Naughty Little Red.*

The valet opened the door. "Welcome back, Mr Saint-Claire."

"Thank you." Stirling offered his arm to Cassie, regretting that he hadn't seen fit to get her a fur, something exquisitely luxurious. "Shall we, my dear?"

She accepted, her hand light on his arm, and yet he was painfully aware of her warmth through his dress jacket, the featherlight weight of her touch. "Of course."

A flash of his Cercle Monte-Carlo card was enough to gain them admittance into the inner sanctum of the salons super-prives—the super private rooms—that only the wealthiest and highly connected would ever see the interior of.

"I feel like I'm stepping back in time," Cassie said in a hushed, awed voice, staring around at the opulence enveloping them. Underneath the warm glow of the bohemian crystal chandeliers, she'd never looked more lovely—at least not in the week and a bit since he'd met her. Had it really only been a matter of days since the saucy little author had sashayed into his life? "I knew it would be over-the-top luxury, but—" She gestured, lost for words at the lavish decorations, the sculptures and paintings, the heavy gold accents.

"The wealthy like a suitable setting to sparkle, and they can't do that if the venue is drab. It just wouldn't do."

"Is that Veronica Hughes?" she whispered, eyes wide as she did her best not to outright stare at the acclaimed actress.

Stirling sent a nod of greeting in the actress's direction. "It is. Would you like to meet her?"

He might have offered her a unicorn from the way her expression stilled, her chest barely rising as if the breath had left her body. "You know her?" She rubbed at her temple. "Of course you do," she muttered. "Because that's totally normal in your universe."

"Is that a yes or no?"

"I wouldn't know what to say," she stammered, hunching her shoulders forward. "And I don't think she'd want to meet a little nobody like me."

Stirling put his hands on her shoulders in a possessive gesture and turned her until he had her full attention. His Little Red. "You, Cassandra Pearson, are not a nobody, of which you took great delight in telling me when we first met. You are a stunningly beautiful and accomplished woman in your own right. Anyone that you consider worthy of spending your time with should consider themselves lucky, and I don't ever want to hear another word about it again. Otherwise, I might have to take steps."

He could feel her body shiver beneath his hands. "What steps?" she said in a husky voice.

"I'm not sure, but I can assure you that I'm rather innovative when I need to be."

Cassie bit down on her bottom lip. "Oh."

"Also, Veronica is one of the nicest people you'll ever meet. Her management can be hard work, but she's genuinely lovely." He looked back to where the actress had been standing moments earlier to disappointedly find that she'd moved to another room. "Maybe next time. Now, Little Red, have you ever played baccarat?"

She shook her head. "Never."

He let his hands drop from her shoulders before taking her hand and once again securely tucking it into the nook of his arm. "Well, I believe that's all about to change."

"Won't it be horrendously expensive to gamble in these rooms?" She looked past him to the guests who sat at the tables.

"Stupendously. And that's what makes it such delicious fun." He leaned in close, inhaling the intoxicating fragrance of her perfume. It was a heady combination of rose and jasmine with warmer woody notes, sandalwood and vanilla and a myriad of others that tickled the edges of his senses. It was a perfect fit for her. "The trick is to decide on an amount for the night, and once it's gone, the night is over."

"Yeah, I did that the few times I went with my mom to Las Vegas. We agreed to one hundred dollars a night."

The innocence with which she made her statement made him want to chuckle until he saw how very serious she was and he quickly squashed the urge for fear of hurting her feelings. "How about you let me worry about the limit tonight."

"But I don't even know how to play," she protested. "What if I lose all the money?"

Gah, she was cute, her face all scrunched up as she worried about money. "You probably will lose money. Baccarat isn't exactly a game of skill, no matter what the player may tell you. It's pure luck." He led her over to a table "All you have to do is bet on any hand before the hand begins."

"But how do I know what the hand is?"

"You don't. Hence why I said it's pure luck. Now, there's a player hand and a bank hand. The game begins with two cards being dealt to each of the hands."

Cassie nodded, her eyes serious as she scrutinized the action on the green velvet table. "So far it sounds easy enough, but what are they betting on?"

"They are predicting which of the hands will acquire a

total that is closest to nine. Other than the hands, they can also bet on the round finishing on a tie." He waved to a passing attendant. "I want one hundred thousand dollars in chips to begin with." Then he put his black Amex down on the tray.

"Stirling, that's too much." Cassie's eyes were huge in shock. "That's a lot of money to just throw away."

"Have I taught you nothing about the billionaire lifestyle?" he admonished. "Everything is bigger, larger. That hundred thousand to me is what the hundred dollars was to you, or more likely what ten dollars is to you. Enjoy it." He turned his attention back to the waiting man. "Can you bring the chips back to the young lady?"

"Yes, sir," the man answered smartly before hurrying away.

Stirling watched him go, catching sight of a familiar figure. "Cassie, when the chips come, get the croupier to deal you in or place your bets. There's someone I need to talk to."

She smiled up at him, albeit a little nervously. "Okay."

He reached out and tenderly stroked her cheek. "You'll be fine. All I want you to do is enjoy yourself." Stirling moved away, his jaw tightening as he approached his quarry at the other table. "Freddy, how long have you been here?"

His friend blinked up at his sudden appearance, a glass of scotch resting beside his hand. "Hello, old chap, I didn't know you were going to be here." He waved his hand languidly. "Deal him in."

"No, thanks," Stirling declined to the croupier. "Freddy, you didn't answer the question. How long have you been here?"

"It's really hard to tell. What day is it?" Freddy's eyes returned hungrily to the game at hand, feverish in their intensity.

"Wednesday."

"Oh, then only a few days, old chap." His friend didn't look up at him, too intent on the cards.

"Weren't you here last week?"

"I believe you're right."

"Freddy, it's becoming a bit of a habit."

Freddy glared at his intrusion. "How about you leave me alone? I'm still winning more than I'm losing," he answered in a clipped, tight voice. "Don't you have that little author project to look after? If I'm not mistaken, she's just at the other table—winning."

Stirling looked over his shoulder to where Cassie was excitedly clapping and chattering with the other players. Every eye was on her, and she shone brighter than any chandelier in the place. "And I'll get back to her in due course. Are you going to tell me what's wrong?"

Freddy threw a chip on the table, watching the other players' reactions. His nostrils flared as they met it and then raised. "Nothing going on. At least nothing new. I can't save my sister from making bad decisions, and when I try, she doesn't want anything to do with me. But that has nothing to do with being here." He threw his cards on the table in disgust. "I like to gamble. So stop with the third degree. It's not like I need to be anywhere or anyone needs me."

Stirling felt his stomach tighten at the bleakness in Freddy's voice. This wasn't like his happy-go-lucky friend, but clearly he didn't want to talk, at least not tonight. But that didn't mean Stirling was going to let it drop, not by a long shot. He clapped his friend on the shoulder. "Well, I need my best friend. You and I have to stick together, what with Landon and Alistair losing their minds and getting married."

Freddy shuddered. "I get nightmares thinking about them. What a waste." He focused his attention on the game again as a new hand was dealt. "Now, get back to your project before someone else swoops in."

He glared, frowning at an Italian count flirting with Cassie and her breathlessly giggling at whatever he'd said. "Can't leave her alone for a second." With long purposeful strides, he strode off to remind Little Red whose arm she belonged on. The Big Bad Wolf. And if that meant biting a few Italian counts, so be it.

I'VE NEVER SEEN anything that comes close to Monaco. In the rooms of the Casino de Monte-Carlo, accents from all around the world spoke, their owners dripping in the trappings of their wealth. Everyone was impeccably dressed as if the shopping there only catered to billionaires and, at worst, millionaires. The streets that I did see were pristine, not a single piece of trash or sign of poverty. Are there poor people in Monaco? Tonight, I won twenty-five thousand dollars, but considering I started with one hundred thousand, not exactly the best night. Dinner at the Monte-Carlo Bay were dishes of caviar, barbajuan, manioc and truffle. I don't know what was better—the food or the people watching.

Interesting note: I never realized the casino was more than just a casino. As well as the seven different salons, it also had seven restaurants. The wine cellar alone holds over six hundred thousand bottles. There was also a country club with twenty-one clay courts, two squash courts, an eighteen-hole golf course and a beach club. WOW! In my wildest imaginations, I couldn't have made up today.

I also met the most charming Italian count. His tales were absolutely fascinating until Stirling bored down on us like a storm cloud and sent poor Silviano scuttling away. The way Stirling looks at me sometimes feels dangerous for how long we've known each other. It scares me how much I want him to keep looking at me like that.

CHAPTER 9

It wasn't like Cassie had never done a celebrity tour of the Hollywood Hills, marveling at the fortresses perched on the slopes or wondering what was behind the private gated streets. It was entirely different to driving those same streets in a town car, wondering which impossibly imposing mansion was Stirling's.

Rubbing her sun-kissed arms, it was hard not to pinch herself. Private jets, superyachts, helicoptering around the French Riviera, it was all just everyday life since she'd met Stirling. She peeked at him from under sooty eyelashes. The man was devilishly handsome, combined with his commanding presence and, let's be honest, swoon-worthy British accent. A romance writer couldn't get a better male love interest. Which begged the question—she knew the reasons he'd given her as to why he'd proposed their fake relationship, but why had he really? Surely he wasn't starved for female company, and it wasn't like she was the type rich billionaires were fighting to have on their arm.

The car pulled smoothly through the gates of a mansion to their left, stopping in front of a large door. From here it looked like most of the house was built going down the side of the hill. Stepping out into the evening air, a sense of curiosity had excitement bubbling away in her belly. This wasn't like the villa in Cannes. This was his home—well, one of them. What would it tell her about Stirling?

As if reading her mind, he smiled that darkly sensuous smirk that was somehow mischievous and arrogant all at the same time. "Home sweet home." He unlocked the door. "I have a house cleaner who comes during the day and makes sure there's food in the pantry and refrigerator for me. Usually when I'm here, I like to spend my time alone in the evenings, especially after a day of dealing with studio heads and actors. I also eat out alone."

It saddened Cassie to think of Stirling sitting in a dark mansion all by himself. It also crossed her mind that maybe he might not want her here. She was just about to say something when she stepped through the door.

"Am I standing on an actual glass bridge?" she squealed, what looked to be a pool lit a glorious blue color below her. "To get from your front door to the rest of the house, THERE'S A BRIDGE!"

Stirling looked a little uncomfortable at her reaction—or maybe it was the bridge? "Yes, and you can blame Freddy for that one."

"Freddy? What does he have to do with it?" Her face scrunched up.

"We were bored one night, so we decided to have a game of upsie."

"What's upsie? Or do I not want to know?"

He grinned at her. "It's nothing bad, although now you make me want it to be all sorts of naughty." Cassie's belly flip-flopped at the searing gaze he sent her way. "Upsie is when you take a balloon and take turns hitting it. The only rule is that it needs to stay up in the air and not touch anything." He stepped off the bridge. "I lost, but there was no way I could have known how cutthroat he was going to be about it."

"So, he bet a glass bridge if you lost, what did you wager?"

"Him sitting for a nude painting class."

"Wow, you guys really are something else."

Stirling winked at her. "I'd like to think I am, at the very least. Freddy, well, he's a lost cause." He threw his arms expansively into the air. "What do you think?" Before she could answer, a sharp ring of his phone interrupted. Stirling glanced down at it, his brows furrowing. "Hold that thought. I need to get this." He left the room.

Cassie had come to LA a few times for book signing events and to get inspiration. Walking to the edge of the glass wall—the whole house seemed to be made of giant expanses of glass—she could only stare transfixed at the vision laid before her. The entry room she stood in seemed to be the narrow hall that connected the two halves of the house, both sides wrapping around a water feature and pool before spilling over the edge against a backdrop of the city lights below. It gave the impression that somehow the house was floating. She could make out Downtown and West LA and all the way to what she presumed was Santa Monica. *If tomorrow is a clear day, I wonder if I'll be able to see the Pacific and Catalina Island.*

"Sorry," Stirling said, returning. "Once they know you're in town, the calls start."

"I was pretty amazed that you didn't get any calls when we were in Cannes."

He gave a half smile, softening the intensity in his eyes. "That's because I asked Angie to handle all my calls." The smolder in his gaze sent a flicker of fire heating her belly in response. "I wanted to be able to give you my full attention. Do you feel special, Little Red?"

He radiated a vitality that drew her like a magnet, and she was by no means blind to his attractions. "I'm feeling something." Such an attraction was dangerous.

The very air around them seemed to be electrified. "Only something?" He lightly fingered a loose tendril of hair on her cheek. "Are you telling me that's the best a New York Bestselling Author can come up with? I'm a little disappointed." He trailed a finger down her jawline, finishing at her trembling lips. "Maybe I need to try harder."

Words, something, something. Her mind had gone blank, her entire being held captive to the trance Stirling had woven around her. Somehow she needed to pull herself back from the perilous edge she'd strayed to. "I'm a little tired from our flight. Would you mind showing me to my room?"

His gaze deepened. "Is that an invitation?"

It took every fiber of her willpower to put her hands on his chest, only to find that she could feel his hard muscles through the fabric. Swallowing hard, she pushed him away. "No, it's actually the complete opposite. If anything, it's me putting up a roadblock to"—she gestured back and forth between them—"whatever this is."

Stirling's mouth twitched before a wry smile graced it. "Purely business then?"

"Yes, the whole boyfriend-girlfriend thing is purely business, and we need to keep it that way." Cassie's knees were turning to jelly, and she prayed he couldn't feel her resolve weakening.

"I understand. I'm not a fan of your decision, but I respect it. At least until I can change your mind." He turned smoothly away. "If you'll follow me, I'll show you to your room. Tomorrow, you'll enter the next stage of your billionaire research. Operation Take Over Tinseltown."

◝

IN A CITY where celebrity was king, Stirling was one better. He was a mover and shaker–one of the shadowy figures in the background who could make or break a career. Sure, you had agents and studio heads, but he was the man who was brought in at the very beginning when the real decisions were being made. He was the one who could turn an errand boy into an in-demand scriptwriter, that unheard of waitress into a star. Stirling had never wanted fame. It was power that had always driven him.

Stepping onto the curb, Stirling buttoned his tailored jacket, his eyes protected from the glare of the sun and passersby by his sunglasses. Satisfied, he opened the door of the Bugatti, watching as the gorgeous woman stepped out into the bright morning sunlight. "Welcome to Rodeo Drive, Little Red."

He smiled politely to a passing group of wives and girl-friends. They were unmistakable in their natural habitat of Beverly Hills. Teetering on impossibly high, red-soled heels, everything primped, pumped, and altered until they all had the same stamp to their features. The women whispered among themselves as they passed, turning to look over their shoulders to stare at Cassie. And not in a friendly way either. Cassie radiated health and vitality as opposed to their cold calculating presence. Stirling tilted his head, gazing at her as she stared around. He could almost hear her mind clicking away as she took mental pictures to write down later in her notepad. Hopefully he would get her out of Hollywood before she morphed into one of them.

"It seems to have all the same shops as when we went shopping in London and what I saw in Monaco." Disappointed, her bottom lipped pouted.

"The explanation is simple," he said, offering her his arm. "Wealthy people are often quite paranoid. They like habit and routine. Sure, they jet-set all around the world, but when they reach their destination, they like to be greeted by the familiar. The same wine, Champagne, favorite food, and of course"—he gestured grandiosely about—"shopping."

"I feel disloyal in saying this, but I think I liked Saint-Tropez the best. I know a lot of the shops were the same, but there was a different vibe around it. Here it seems harder, colder."

"That's because here the only substance you have is how much money you have, how much power and influence, and if you happen to be a woman who doesn't possess the first, the currency of your beauty."

Cassie sighed forlornly. "I thought a billionaire romance would be shiny and glamourous, but I actually feel a little depressed right now." She rubbed her arms, staring at her reflection in the window, outfits worth more than average people earned in a month closeted inside. "I'm standing in front of Chanel on Rodeo Drive and I'm feeling depressed. That can't be normal."

Stirling came closer, looking at the reflection of them as a couple. It seemed right. "You'd be surprised how often people are wandering about this street feeling doom and gloom. Of course, with all the Botox, it's hard to tell. But I've never heard of anyone being depressed inside the shops spending money."

"I'm not sure that's true." She grinned up at him, turning away from the window.

"When was the last time you tried?" he teased her.

"Well, the first and only time I've been shopping at Chanel was in London and I wasn't depressed then. At least, not the second time when I had your black credit card."

"Then you're not qualified to answer the question." His arm came firmly around her waist, pulling her in closer to his side, her intoxicating fragrance catching him in its snare. "I propose that we put it to the test."

Cassie rolled her eyes as she laughed. "I'm not sure we have to test it."

"What kind of researcher do you take me for?" he said in mock indignation. "Certainly not the kind to do research and do only half the job. Chin up, Little Red. We shall soldier on and get our answers."

"Yes, sir." Cassie gave him a sharp salute.

Heat pooled in his stomach. "I like it when you call me sir."

"I would suggest not getting used to it," she said tartly, brow quirked in a challenge as they entered the luxurious store.

The room with all its polished surfaces, glass and mirrors should feel cold. Instead, Stirling was feeling decidedly warm. "I like proving people wrong, too."

"Then I hope you like disappointment." Her cheeks flushed. Was she feeling the heat between them as well?

"Cassie, I've experienced a lot of things since I met you. Disappointment has never been one of them."

Something shimmered in her eyes, but with all the good timing of a pimple on your nose just before prom, the sales attendant chose that exact moment to be of assistance. "Can I help you today?" Her gaze wavered between the two of them, her eyes sharpening when she recognized him. *Most likely a sales assistant/waitress/actress/singer.*

"The young lady needs a cure for her melancholy."

"Stirling," Cassie said in a warning voice. She turned apologetically to the other woman. "You'll have to excuse him. He thinks he's much funnier than he is. It's best not to encourage it though, as then he's impossible." She smiled sweetly at him, but he could see the challenge in the depths of her eyes.

Challenge accepted. "You give me no choice." He prowled

closer. "If shopping won't fix your feeling down, then I'll have to resort to what I know will definitely chase it away."

The defiance died in her eyes, chased away by apprehension, but it didn't stop her from swallowing hard and raising her stubborn little chin to meet his gaze. "Whatever it is, don't even think about it."

"Too late." He swooped forward, hearing the shocked twitter of the sales assistant as he swept Cassie into his arms and began to rain butterfly light kisses all over her face.

A delicious giggle tinkled from Cassie as she squirmed. "I give up," she finally managed in a breathless voice.

"Do you feel better?" He still held her close, noting her dilated pupils and heightened color with satisfaction.

"Yes."

"Maybe I should give you a few more, just to be on the safe side. After all, I don't want to do only half the job."

"Yes, I'm sure. I feel better." She laid the palms of her hands flat on his chest, obviously in preparation to push him away. *But only if I let her.*

"Excellent." Stirling stepped back. "Now, to really make sure, I think you still need a spot of retail therapy." He gave a bored look at the sales assistant. "If you would be so kind."

"I'll take care of your girlfriend, Mr Saint-Claire."

"Excellent." Pulling his phone from his pocket, he took a plush seat near the change lounge. "And Cassie?"

"Yes?"

"Remember to live the billionaire life."

"I'll get your meals out to you when they're ready." The waitress directed her words to Stirling, seemingly not caring if Cassie had an opinion on anything.

"Thank you." Stirling reached for his glass and, perhaps feeling the burn of her glare, he looked at Cassie. "What?"

"Nothing." She followed his cue and reached sullenly for her own wine.

"Take it from someone who knows what he's talking about. You're not much of an actress. What got you all poopy-faced?"

Cassie's mouth dropped open. *He did not just call me poopy-faced!* "Geeze, thanks."

"Stirling, I didn't know you were back in town. The last I heard you were having a break from LA." She turned to find herself staring at the aging visage of one Mason Cooper. When she'd been growing up, he'd been her mother's favorite movie star.

"Mason, you know how it is. I needed to recharge, but then I missed the action of Hollywood," Stirling answered easily. "Are you working?"

"I'm between projects at the moment. Actually, I was sent a script that I think my son, Kirk, and I would be great for. You know, really capitalize on the father-son thing."

"The last I heard, Kirk was booked out for at least six movies. That and he's taking on fewer roles now that his lovely wife, Ash, has had the baby."

"Money talks. With the right persuasion, I'm sure he'll come around." There was an unappealing note of desperation in the aging actor's voice.

"I wish you luck with that, but I'm here for pleasure not business today." Stirling indicated Cassie sitting across the table from him.

Mason looked her up and down, leaving her feeling like a cold piece of meat. "I thought she was your assistant. Not your usual taste for fun."

Cassie's top lip curled disdainfully, a scorching retort hot on her lips. But before she could set fire to the rude jerk's innards, Stirling smoothly stepped up to the plate. "You're right, she's not my usual type." She wanted to kick him in the shins for his betrayal. "This is my girlfriend, Cassie." Transfixed, she watched a gamut of emotions chase themselves across Mason's face. *Surely it wasn't healthy to have such a splotchy complexion.*

Mason gave her a smug smirk. "She must have something going for her to last longer than the rest." Cassie fought the urge to depart from the table immediately in search of a bleach bath.

"I suggest you leave before you destroy what little career you have left." The words were firm, but it was the ominous, set expression on Stirling's face that was terrifying. Mason obviously agreed, scuttling away without another word.

"Well, he's an odious toad," Cassie said scathingly.

"You have no idea. Even his own son wants nothing to do with him."

"I can see why."

"People like him are a dime a dozen. You'll get used to it, especially when we go on set."

"We?"

"Of course. There's no way I'm leaving my girlfriend's side whom I adore more than life itself. She must accompany me." Stirling rested his chin on his hand and fluttered his eyelashes as he stared in faux adoration at her.

She gave a light laugh and took a sip of wine, hoping it would stop the butterflies dancing in her belly. It was silly to feel so giddy around him when he'd never asked her once how she felt about him. The wine turned sour in her mouth. In this town, it seemed like all the power was firmly held in the hands of men.

～

*I*T WAS SAID IN JEST, *but somehow I have become a commodity. Stirling is in charge, and I have become subservient to him. He has decided I will come onto sets with him, and he did not ask me. I am the girlfriend, no longer Cassie, a person in her own right. I have not once been asked what I do, everyone seemingly basing my worth on that of being attached to Stirling. This, it seems, is the only thing that matters. For the record, this will not be what happens to my heroine!*

CHAPTER 10

The security guard waved them through the boom gate, not even bothering to ask for ID. The perks of being a heavy hitter in Hollywood, Cassie guessed as they passed under the decorative arches spanning over the entrance. The movie lot was enclosed by a high perimeter wall. *I wonder how effective it really is against stalkers and the paps.* Inside, it was a bustling village of buildings ranging from smaller single-story offices to huge sound stages and everything in between.

"This place is humungous," she said, completely unprepared for the scale of the studio lot.

Stirling grinned at her as he pulled up in front of a building proudly bearing the signage *Saint-Claire Productions inc.* "I'll take you on a tour once I check in with my assistant and see if there is anything urgent I need to attend to. I think you'll like life on the lot." *Life on the lot.* It certainly buzzed with a certain energy as she emerged from the car and followed Stirling through the door.

"Hello, Mr Saint-Clare," the brightly dressed male receptionist greeted Stirling as he walked past.

"Hello, Lewis. You look like you enjoyed your break in Florida." Stirling rested an elbow on the high-gloss reception counter.

"It did wonders for my tan and my love life." He winked conspiratorially at his boss. Curious, he glanced at Cassie. "Angie didn't tell me you were bringing in new talent today. Hello, gorgeous."

"Hi, I'm not new talent," she said hesitantly.

"Oh, honey. I know everyone in these parts and if I've never met you, you are definitely new," Lewis said with a dramatic snap of his fingers.

"What Cassie is trying to say is that, although I can see why you think she would be talent, she is actually my girlfriend." Stirling reached out and touched her hand, giving it a little squeeze.

"Good for you, girlfriend. And Mr Saint-Clare, you be nice to this one. I like her already."

Stirling's mouth quirked as he gave Cassie an enigmatic glance out of the corner of his eye. "I like this one, too." Her heart flip-flopped at the casually uttered words. "Is Angie in yet?"

"Have you ever known Angie to be late?" Lewis sassed.

"No."

"Then Angie is here."

Cassie covered her mouth to stifle the giggles that threatened to erupt. Clearly Stirling's staff were not intimidated by him.

Rolling his eyes at Cassie, Stirling strode off, muttering good-naturedly under his breath. "Good help is so hard to get in LA."

"I heard you, Mr Saint-Claire, and don't think for one minute that you don't have the best receptionist in LA. The offers I knock back out of sheer loyalty to you is positively obscene," Lewis called.

"Lewis is awesome," Cassie said.

"Don't let him hear you. You've met him. Do you think he needs an ego boost?" Stirling smiled broadly as they came to a desk set up outside a door with his name on it. "Angie, have you settled back into life in LA?"

"Stirling, it's the same work I do regardless of where you would have us work from," the woman said dryly. "I think even my desk is the same between offices."

"That's not really that imaginative, Stirling," Cassie chastised.

"Angie's the one who selected the final décor for our offices," Stirling protested. "I only signed off on it."

"What can I say? I'm a creature of habit." Angie smiled at Cassie. "Speaking of habits, it's nice to see you again."

"Same." She wondered what had been said between Angie and her boss about her since she'd last seen the assistant. *Probably nothing.*

"I read your book and really loved it. It has all the elements to make a fantastic movie and, for what it's worth, I really hope we make it." Cassie felt herself grow warm under the assistant's praise. Every book she wrote was one of her babies and nothing made her happier than when a reader enjoyed it.

"Angie's the one who brought your book to my attention and she's never steered me wrong yet." Stirling captured her eyes with his. "Maybe we might just have to see about making it a reality."

Cassie's breath caught in her throat. She'd had books optioned before. The initial elation at the possibility that one of her books would be brought to the big screen, the fading hope as time went on, and the realization that it wasn't going to happen. *I wonder if he's just saying it, dangling the promise to get into my good books.* She liked to think he wasn't. The proof would be in the movie.

"I WASN'T sure what I was expecting, but not this mini city." Cassie's head didn't stop moving as she took it all in. Stirling tilted his head so he could steal a glance at her while he also tried to keep an eye on pedestrians and other drivers as he drove his personal golf cart around the lot.

"It's more than just sound stages and offices." He gestured expansively around them before taking the opportunity to rest it on the backrest of Cassie's seat. "We're just passing the studio commissary, for example."

"The what?"

"It's our cafeteria. You'll find everything required for production and postproduction on this lot." He took in a deep breath. "Sound studios, props, costumes, cameras, sound recording, crafts, sets, lighting, makeup rooms, rehearsal rooms, backlots, special effects, cutting, editing, scoring, rerecording. The entire dream factory in one location." Stirling didn't think he would ever lose the thrill he felt at being part of making movies. "On a side note, you see that water tower up there?" He pointed to one in the distance.

She scrunched up her face, peering under the roof of the cart. "Yeah, water towers seem to be a movie thing somehow."

"That's because nitrate film was manufactured and used until 1951 and was highly flammable. That was before you added a lot of sets and backlots that were also highly flammable and that's why most studio lots built in the early to mid-twentieth century have water towers—to help with fire-fighting efforts."

"I did not know that," Cassie admitted. "But that's not saying much. I'm really over my head with all this movie stuff."

"Just stick with me, doll face, and I'll look after you," he said in his best Bronx accent.

Cassie giggled. "That accent was atrocious."

"All the better, doll."

As Stirling continued to drive around the lot pointing out attractions and famous people, he found he rather enjoyed having a girlfriend. Obviously, it would be nice to have someone to snuggle up with at the end of each night, but this fake girlfriend was the best relationship he'd ever been in.

Maybe that said more than he'd like about his past relationships.

CHAPTER 11

For two weeks Cassie had spent every day down at the studio lot soaking it all in. It really was amazing the doors that opened as soon as they found out she was Stirling's girlfriend. Was it possible to both love and hate the idea of being called that? The way he looked at her—heck, the way that gorgeous man looked, full stop—and the weird friendship that they'd struck sometimes made her wish there was more to the relationship than a false label designed to enable her to get the research she needed for her billionaire romance. But then when her worth as a person was weighed up solely as being the girlfriend of Stirling, that any achievements or accomplishments she had were tied up to who she was with, that rankled her, twisting in her gut until she felt like she wanted to throw up.

"Heck, I hope that sour look isn't because of me," Stirling said from his desk where she'd been unconsciously watching him from her perch on the luxurious black leather sofa, her pen hovering forgotten over her notepad.

Cassie was humiliatingly conscious of his scrutiny as he

waited expectantly, folding his arms together as he continued to look at her. "Don't you think that's a little arrogant?"

"To have the belief that you're thinking about me"—Stirling gave her a lopsided smirk—"or that I actually asked?"

She could feel her cheeks flame hotly. Cassie chose to believe it was because of his high-handed manner, not because he was uncomfortably close to the truth. "Well, this expression right here"—she circled her face in the air—"is pure you."

"In that case, I better make sure I get myself back into your good books. What would you say if I told you that I've decided to move forward with the production of your book?"

Her breath slammed out of her body. None of her books had ever progressed past the optioning stage before. This might actually be happening. Her story might end up on the big screen for everyone to see. "I don't even know what the next step is. This is officially uncharted territory for me."

"We start getting a script in place. That is a whole process all by itself, which I'm sure you're going to find out about since you're part of the process, one I hope will include you wanting to be part of writing that script, since I'm going to give you a contract that says as much."

She raised stunned eyes to his faintly amused one, like he'd known how she'd react to the news he had just calmly delivered. "I just assumed that maybe I'd get invited once or twice to be on set and that would be it." A tremor ran through her voice at the realization that she didn't have to give control of her story—her baby—away. "I can't believe it."

"Believe it." He abruptly planted his palms on his desk and pushed himself upright. "Now, I need to go check on the wardrobe fitting for one of our upcoming movies."

"Is that something you normally look after?" Cassie rose to follow him. "I just assumed it would be someone else's responsibility."

"The buck stops with me, and when there are millions of bucks at stake each and every time we put a movie together, I like to make sure I know how things are traveling so I can correct for any deviations that will cost time and money down the track." He held the door open for her. "And I think you'll get a kick out of this."

She looked suspiciously at him over the rim of her glasses. "Why?"

"Trust me."

Cassie stared doubtfully at his back as he sauntered down the hall. "I don't like the sound of that."

Stirling's laugh rumbled back to her. "Oh, ye of little faith. You have to trust me at some point."

She hurried to catch up. "I'm not at that point yet."

"Yet," he pointed out. "You said yet, and I'm going to keep you to that."

"IT'S VERONICA HUGHES." Cassie tugged urgently on his sleeve as she whispered furiously. "You didn't tell me it was Veronica Hughes."

It was entirely possible that Cassie was about to go into cardiac arrest given the state she was in. *Her heart might not last in Hollywood at this rate.* "Be cool. Veronica is a sweetheart." He put an arm around her, surprised that she was actually shaking. "Veronica, gorgeous as usual." He bussed her cheek, pulling Cassie forward as he did so.

"It helps with the costumes they've created for me," the actress said in her signature low husky voice. She looked curiously at the dumbstruck author under his arm. "I'd heard you had a girlfriend." Veronica held out an elegant hand to Cassie. "It's a pleasure to meet you. And I must say, you must be one tough lady if you've got this one eating out of the palm of your hand." She sent Stirling a teasing smile, only enough to touch her eyes without crinkling her skin. "Many have tried and failed."

Cassie brightened under the warmth of Veronica's welcome. At least she'd stopped trembling. "Oh, it's been remarkably easy so far, and I know you must get this all the time, but I'm a huge fan." Cassie pressed her lips together, color flooding her cheeks. "And now I sound like a real idiot and not cool at all."

Veronica's beautifully rich laughter filled the awkward silence as Cassie appeared to do her level best to disappear into her shoes. "Cassie, I wouldn't be able to do what I do or live the life I have without fans. I'm so glad you like my work."

"I'm a writer, and Stirling is producing one of my books into a movie, and I know you would be perfect for one of the characters. It's set in World War II, and it's about the women who flew airplanes between the fields, often in bad conditions. Some even lost their lives," Cassie blurted, the words tumbling over themselves as they left her mouth in a great flurry.

"I would certainly love to read for the part," the actress replied graciously, turning her head when an assistant began to beckon her over. "It was a pleasure to meet you, Cassie, and Stirling, I really would like to hear more about this movie."

"I'll make sure I get a script to your agent when we have something." Stirling gave Cassie a little squeeze. *She might not be built for Tinseltown—she was too genuine—but heck if he wasn't proud of her passion.*

"Thank you." With a flurry of feathers and chiffon, she was gone.

"Is it wrong that I somehow feel like I just met a

unicorn?" Cassie whispered, eyes as big as saucers staring up at him from behind her glasses.

Man, she was cute. "Well, there is a certain magic to it all." He led her back out the door and toward his car. He'd done more than enough today, and there was a beautiful woman he wanted to spend some time spoiling.

Cassie bit her lip, turning away from him, but not before he could see the dullness of uncertainty in her eyes. "You are progressing with my book." She hesitated when she reached the car before turning to face him, the sun bright on her face. "Is it because of us?" She tortured her bottom lip again. "I mean, us isn't real, but is it because of that?"

The question hung in the air between them. *Was it?* He gently stroked her face. For his benefit or hers, he wasn't sure. "I didn't make billions from being stupid. I'm going forward with production because it's a sound business decision." *And it gives me a reason to have you around longer.*

"Oh, that makes sense." Was it his imagination, or did that sound a little flat? *Was she disappointed? Did she want a them—a real them?*

A sense of urgency drove him, the need to find out. Cassie gazed at him, a question of her own shining brightly from her eyes. It was too easy to get lost in the way she looked at him. His blood coursing through his veins like an awakened river, he swept her weightlessly in his arms. The time for chaste bedtime kisses was gone as he plundered her willing lips with his own. *Maybe the question was answered after all.*

CHAPTER 12

How did I get here? It was like Cassie had fallen down the rabbit hole and ended up as the main character in her own romance book. Stirling Saint-Claire—billionaire movie producer, British hottie and all-round thirst trap—was her boyfriend. Like, real boyfriend, not pretend. Each day she'd come to work with him, setting herself up on the sofa in his office. Some days they drove around the lot and he introduced her to people, other days he was in and out of meetings and she hardly saw him at all. But each night he'd spend with her, either out to dinner or parties or at home snuggled up on the sofa, gazing at the lights of LA below them.

"This is starting to become a bit of a habit," Stirling said, throwing a devastating smirk her way. "Not that I'm complaining."

Cassie drank it all in—his compelling eyes, the firm features, the confident set of his shoulders. *It was enough to give a lady crazy thoughts.* "You love it."

"Won't deny that. But if you're finished admiring my perfection, we have a meeting to get to."

She stared at his enigmatic expression for a moment longer. "A meeting I need to attend?" Cassie left the question hanging. Why did she need to go?

"Yes." He quirked mischievous brows at her. "I think you might want to meet the scriptwriter you'll be working with."

"The scriptwriter I'll be working with?" she repeated dumbly. Her eyes flew wide open. "You mean you're starting the script? On my book?" Her voice rose higher with each word she uttered. *It was actually starting to happen.*

"Technically I'm not doing anything. You and Zayne will be doing all the work. I just plan on taking the credit for discovering such an amazing new talent and delivering her to the world." She shivered under the intensity of his gaze. "Now, are you planning on keeping your co-scriptwriter waiting all day or not?"

With a little shriek, Cassie threw herself into his arms and planted kisses on his gorgeous face. "Thank you, thank you, thank you."

"Don't thank me yet. You haven't met Zayne or started doing all the hard work of getting it done," Stirling admonished gently, accepting the kisses as his due.

"I know it'll be perfect."

"WHAT DO YOU CALL THIS?" The large, pale man threw the offending papers down in front of her, his jowls quivering in indignation.

Cassie stared down at the title emblazoned on it in bold type. *War Brides, a novel by Cassandra Pearson.* "My book. Or at least a printout of it and some notes I made. Just some ideas I had." Why did her voice sound so small?

"How about this?" His small eyes narrowed on her, reminding her of a pig. "You make the coffee."

"I can go get us coffee before we start." Cassie jumped up, grabbing her bag.

"I don't think you understand. I don't want you to get coffee for us, what I want is for you to get coffee and stay out of my way while I do what I do best. Write great scripts."

She stared at him, the breath leaving her body in a great whoosh as his words hit her. All the excitement and pride she'd been feeling was gone in a snap of his fleshy fingers. "But I wrote the book." Cassie managed no more than a broken, hoarse whisper of protest.

"And it was a good attempt, but let the pro handle it from here." Zayne's words were loaded with ridicule.

Knowing that, if she didn't leave the room, she'd start crying in front of him—and that would be worse than how she was feeling now—she slunk from the room, her tail well and truly between her legs.

"How was your first day working on the script?" Stirling passed a glass of wine to Cassie. He couldn't wait to hear how her first hands-on movie making experience had gone. *I wonder if she catches the bug the same way I did.*

"It's a very different process from writing my books." Cassie took a long drink, staring out over the city lights. "I'm not sure what I thought it would be like."

"Zayne is one of the best in the business. Every script he has a hand in turns into box office gold. Investors love seeing his name on the page." It was the reason he'd taken the scriptwriter onboard. He wanted Cassie to learn from the best and for her movie to be a success.

"He's a bit of a big deal, then?" She twisted the stem of her glass around in her hand.

"He's more than a big deal. You've met the man. He's not exactly shy about letting people know that he's the real deal."

Cassie's earnest eyes sought his from behind her glasses. "And he can make sure my book is a great movie?"

"And you a great scriptwriter if you soak up what he has to show you." She was beginning to see the gift he'd given her, how much he wanted to help her be everything she could be.

She gave a sharp nod, as if coming to some sort of decision. A soft smile chased away the contemplation. "So, how was your day, Stirling?"

"Who's Rose?" Cassie stared down at the script in bewilderment.

"I changed Agnes's name. It wasn't particularly marketable." Zayne sipped the coffee Cassie had just brought him.

"But Rose isn't anything like Agnes," she protested. "Agnes was the main character, and now she's pushed into the background as a piece of arm candy for this new male lead. All the women have been pushed into the background." It was like he'd taken the heart out of her book and wiped his feet on it.

"Men won't go to see a movie about a bunch of women and, while I'm at it, the name of the movie needs to be changed. War Brides isn't going to get bums on seats."

"The story is about women during the Second World War who happened to fall in love. Agnes flies planes for Pete's sake, putting her life at risk time and again for the boys flying the missions. She's a heroine, not some blushing flower in the background. The man she falls in love with, that's what he admires and loves about her. They're kindred free spirits, and that's what makes it all the sadder when he's killed. But then you have the comradeship she experiences with Suki, a Japanese war bride, when she returns to normal life. Heck, you've turned Suki into some sort of submissive geisha type and that's not her at all. These are women's stories that deserve to be front and center, not pushed into the background. This"—she jabbed at the manuscript—"isn't my book." The bite of anger made her hands tremble. They couldn't do this to her story!

"I was brought onto this project to do what I do best. Take a mediocre book and turn it into a blockbuster. I suggest you keep doing what you do best." Zayne's flat hard eyes bored into her.

"And what would that be?" Cassie had had enough. No one was going to bastardize her work. Not Zayne, and not Stirling if it came to it. Not while she still had breath.

"You haven't gotten the coffee order wrong yet." He gave her a smarmy smirk. "And you seem to show some talent as far as Mr Saint-Claire is concerned."

"What are you saying exactly?" she ground out, a fine red haze settling over her.

"Stick to what you're good at and let the professionals do their job, sweetie. And in your case, it seems like what you're good at is sleeping with the producer."

Cassie fired him a hostile look, blinded by the searing flash of rage that descended in a red haze over her. "You don't know a thing about me and Stirling," she spat out contemptuously. "And I'm not sleeping with him. I'm not that kind of girl."

"Darling, I'm only reporting what I've heard, and from where I'm sitting, it's the only reason this piece of crap"—he picked up her book from the desk and then dropped it again —"is getting made. It doesn't make sense otherwise."

The pain of her nails digging into her palms anchored her

into the moment, otherwise she feared she would explode into incandescent rage. "That piece of crap was good enough to be a bestseller."

"There must be a lot of bored, old housewives who bought your book." Zayne's expression lost its cruel edge, somehow appearing milder—less threatening—as he returned to tapping away on his computer. "Cassie, I need you to allow me the respect of getting my work done," he said in a harassed voice. "I take my work very seriously, and if you don't have the same work ethic as myself, then I will try to do the best I can for this project, despite the repeated harassment I've received from you. At the very least, do it for Mr Saint-Claire, who has put his name on the line for you."

"Respect?" Cassie choked out. "I have less than zero respect for you. What you have done is an abomination, and honestly, I don't care what Stirling thinks. In fact, I couldn't care less. This was my book before he came along and it will be mine long after he's gone" She knew she was shrieking at him like some sort of crazy woman, but she didn't care. Why had she said after he's gone? Her mouth in its fury was running away on her.

"Careful, Cassie."

She jumped as Stirling's hard voice rumbled over her shoulder. She didn't know how long he'd been there, but relief surged through her. Now he could put Zayne back in his box. "Stirling, I didn't know you were there."

"Obviously." His narrowed eyes were hard, his nostrils flared as he stared at her. *Wait, what?* Why was he mad at her? "Zayne, I apologize for putting you in this position. There are a few things about Cassie I was clearly ignorant about."

"I don't hold you accountable at all." Zayne was all soothed hurt. "Sometimes the ones we care about don't share the same motivation."

"Would you please leave us?" Stirling commanded to the

scriptwriter, still not turning his head to look at Cassie. Her stomach twisted into knots. He was furious at her, but surely he would calm down once she explained it was just a stupid slip of the tongue. Anyway, what Zayne had been doing was way worse.

"Certainly."

She'd never seen the overweight man move so fast. *Hopefully he'll spend the next ten minutes catching his breath*, she thought spitefully. "Stirling, I can explain."

"No, Cassie. I want you to listen. I've done nothing but help you since we met. I've opened doors for you that would have firmly remained close, I've let you into my life, and I've asked for nothing." Stirling's hands clenched and unclenched as he spoke.

Tears sprung into Cassie's eyes at the hurt she could see, hurt she'd caused by careless words spoken in haste. "I know, and you have no idea how much that means to me." *How much you mean to me.*

"I've spent so much time trying to give you everything. The experiences, shopping, making this movie—your movie —into everything it can be, and it's not because I want it for me. I want it for you. But clearly you don't give a darn about what I think." He touched her cheek gently with his knuckle. "That hurts, Cassie. More than I'd like to admit."

"Stirling, I'm sorry. It's not how it sounded."

"I know what I heard," he snapped back. "Don't treat me like I'm stupid."

Cassie jerked back at his tone. "But it's okay for me to be treated like that?"

"When have I ever treated you like that?" His face was so close to hers she could feel the anger as the heat of his words hit her face. "Tell me, Cassie. When?"

"By making me work with Zayne for one."

"By making you work with the best scriptwriter I know in the business? How is that treating you like you're stupid?"

"Yeah, well, he's not that great."

"His track record begs to differ." Stirling took a step away, rubbing the back of his neck in ragged movements. "You need to let go of your ego and listen to what he suggests."

"My ego?" she spat. "I'm amazed that I was even allowed to have one, considering I'm just the girlfriend. Heaven help me if I should have an opinion and worth of my own."

"Is it so bad being my girlfriend?" Stirling snarled, rounding on her. "Trust me, there are plenty of women who are more than happy to fill your place in an instant."

Cassie's anger numbed the pain of her heart shattering into a million pieces. Later, the agony would bleed through her, sapping her of her strength, but for now her spine remained rigid. "Then let them. I have a book conference to go to where I'm the keynote speaker and fans will be lining up for my autograph." It surprised her that her feet moved when she asked them to. She turned and looked at him over her shoulder. "And not one of them will give a darn whose girlfriend I am. All they'll care about is that Cassandra Pearson is there in the flesh." Before her will could give out, she fled from the room and the handsome billionaire who had just broken her heart.

conomy wasn't so bad. It's not like she needed all the extra room that Stirling's private jet had afforded her. She'd never flown anything else but coach before she'd met him, and if he thought she would go to him cap in hand to ask for the use of his plane, he had another thing coming. At least she'd paid for her ticket with her own money. Cassandra Pearson didn't need a man to take care of her. She had her own money and life.

She also collected her own luggage from the baggage carousel, hailed her own taxi and checked into her own hotel room that she'd reserved herself, thank you very much. Tomorrow morning, she'd even set up her own signage and table ready for her book signing. That is, once she got through her keynote speech tonight.

Cassie stared down at the dress she'd packed for the evening. Since she'd met Stirling, she shuddered to think about how much he'd spent on clothing for her and she'd made a point of leaving those outfits behind. The red dress lay stark against the white of the hotel bed linen. Red, the color of love, seemed fitting for her to wear as a romance author up there on stage. The fact it was the most she'd ever spent on a dress before had also weighed into her decision. But now that it was time to put it on, Cassie was having second thoughts. It was impossible to not think about Stirling. She stared down, catching sight of the jeweled panther bracelet, the one item that she hadn't been able to leave behind. Somehow, looking down and seeing the gleaming eyes at her wrist made her feel better, like it was only a lovers' tiff rather than something more serious.

This is ridiculous, it's just a stupid dress. Gritting her teeth, she snatched it off the bed, the fabric whispering against her skin as she stepped into it. Looking at the clock on the bedside table, she muttered a curse under her breath. She'd spent so much time being an idiot over a simple dress that, if she didn't get a wiggle on, she would be late—for her own speech. Struggling to zip it up, she made her way to the bathroom to do her hair.

"WHAT DOES romance look like to me?" *Oh, the irony.* The words stared accusingly up at her. Why had she written this as her conclusion? "It's messy. When I write, I don't want that perfect couple, the perfect life. I want the reader to feel it, for it to be authentic. Yes, it's a fantasy, it has a happy ending, and in real life, that isn't always guaranteed." The words shimmered, and Cassie swallowed over the lump in her throat. "That's why we write romance and why you read it. We escape into a world filled with characters who are just like us. We know in our hearts that we don't belong there, but for that one moment, it's nice to pretend. Pretend that we will get that happily ever after, too."

The applause rose from the dimly lit room in front of her as the audience clapped their approval. Gathering her notes, she quickly bustled from the bright lights of the stage.

"Cassie, I was amazed that you still had time to come to this conference," Stella Reed, fellow romance author and frenemy, said. She planted an air kiss inches from Cassie's cheek.

"Stella, I wouldn't miss it for the world, but why would you doubt that I would be here?" Cassie still felt fragile from her speech.

"Well, now that you're going to have the movie made and all. I see you've finally cracked the code of how to get one's book up on the big screen." The woman was all false friendliness, pure ice underlining each word.

"Write a good book? Is that why you haven't had a movie made?"

"Oh, you are in a funny mood tonight, Cassie." Stella waved off the insult. The woman had a hide like a rhino. "What I meant was just sleep with the producer. Maybe I should try it. I mean, it worked for you. You really did get lucky. He isn't fat, old and ugly like most of them."

Cassie permitted herself a withering glare. "For one, I'm not sleeping with the producer."

"I thought you were together?"

"That doesn't mean I'm sleeping with him. Also"—she gave Stella a disdainful sweep of her gaze—"I find it a little presumptuous that you think you could land a movie producer. You might be desperate to get your book made into a movie, but you can't compete with a starlet desperate to star in a movie. Now, if you'll excuse me, I'm eager for a glass of wine and a long soak in the tub before a full day of signing tomorrow." Regally, she left the other woman to stare at her in offended silence as she swept from the room.

~

"You're not a moment too soon—" The words died on Cassie's lips as she stared at him in disbelief. She was half hidden behind the door, and from what he could see, she was encased in a fluffy bathrobe.

"Who, exactly, were you expecting, Cassie?" Stirling ground out, pushing through the door and into the room, slamming it behind him. "Because I know for a fact you sure as heck weren't expecting me." *He'd flown down here to surprise her. Turns out he was the one getting the surprise. What an idiot.*

"I don't know their name." She crossed her arms over her chest, causing the neckline of her robe to gape. She quickly tugged it shut, and her sleeves fell back, revealing the bracelet he'd given her on her wrist. *How dare she wear that to meet another man.*

"You don't know their name?" Did she just go and pick up a random stranger? He could see it now, her down at the hotel bar in that red dress.

"No, because when I rang room service for a bottle of wine, they didn't tell me who was delivering it." She glared at him with cold flinty eyes. "Is there anything else you want, or did you just come to accuse me of things?"

He felt like a jerk. The last thing he'd meant to do was act like the jealous idiot. He'd come here to try to make things better. "I came here to see you." Cassie didn't seem to be softening at all. "I missed you."

"You have a funny way of showing it." *Definitely not softening.*

"Have you missed me?"

"No one gives me a chance to, since all anyone wants to tell me is that the only reason I'm doing well in life is because I'm Stirling Saint-Claire's girlfriend," she spat at him.

"Why are you so mad at me?"

"Because I'm sick of hearing it."

"You're sick of hearing that you're my girlfriend?" Frustration turned the words mean.

"Don't put words in my mouth. Gah, since I met you, I've lost me. Being seen and valued for being me." She jabbed at her chest. "Cassie Pearson. She might not be rich and fancy, but she is successful, and she was before she'd ever heard your name."

"Well, she can be averagely successful after she's forgotten my name." Anger forced the words from his lips, and pride stopped him from retracting them, even when he saw the flash of hurt in her eyes.

"I really don't think we have much more to say then." Cassie chewed at the inside of her cheek, her gaze sliding away to the hallway wall behind him as she picked at the sleeve of her bathrobe.

"Looks like it." His chest felt like it was being squeezed in a vise, but somehow his voice sounded normal. "We can talk when you come back and hopefully you've calmed down and are being more sensible."

"Because if I'm upset for not being valued for me or, heaven help me, have a different opinion from a man, then I'm not being sensible?" She threw the words at him like one would darts at a board. All of them hitting painfully home. *If she were a man, would he be handling this better? The fact was, he wasn't in love with a man. He was in love with her.* "Can you please get Angie to send my things—the things that are mine, not what you bought for me—to my apartment?"

No. "I can do that. Where is that, exactly?" Somehow the room was darker, or maybe it was his brain being oxygen-starved as he could no longer breath. He plastered a smile on his face. He wasn't going to show how much he was hurting. Stirling Saint-Claire didn't get hurt, not by a woman.

"Boise. I'll send the details to Angie." Her voice broke. *Was she hurting, too?* "Here." She pulled the panther bracelet from her wrist with jerky movements and gave it to him. "Now, can you please go?"

"Cassie, I—" He wasn't going to beg, and he had nothing to apologize for. She'd calm down and come crawling back, and then she'd be the one begging for forgiveness. "You know where to find me." He left and found the outside world was just as dark and airless as the hotel room had been. It was best that she didn't know the power she held over him. He sucked in a breath. *She'd be back, and she never had to know.*

CHAPTER 14

Her mom made the best roast chicken. Cassie picked at the crispy chicken skin with her fingers.

"Cassandra Pearson, manners!" admonished her mother.

Cassie flashed her a cheeky grin as she complied. *It was good to be home.* She'd dropped her things off to her apartment earlier, but there was no way she was going to miss out on a home-cooked meal. Outside she could make out the mountains covered in trees, houses dotted between them. It hit that somehow she always seemed to be somewhere looking out at the mountain vista below.

"Your mother showed me some pictures of your book signing on social media. It looked like there were lots of people waiting for your autograph. I'm proud of you, Cassie," her dad said gruffly. He wasn't the type to give compliments. It wasn't that he didn't care, he just wasn't comfortable with that degree of affection.

This simple man, one that she respected and loved, was proud of her—Cassie—for her achievements. Her chest ached at hearing what her soul had been thirsting for since she'd been on her crazy ride with Stirling. "Thanks, Dad."

"Long?" her mother said, passing the bread around. "They were insane. I think it's because everyone's getting excited that the movie is being made. Which brings me to the next question, when am I going to meet the dashing Stirling Saint-Claire? He's so handsome whenever I see him in the society pages, but I need to find out for myself if he's son-in-law material."

Cassie choked as the chicken went dry in her mouth. "Um, I wouldn't count on him being around anytime soon." *If ever.*

"What happened?" Mom set the bread down and gave her a concerned look.

"We broke up." There, she'd said it. So why did she feel like her heart had dropped to the floor?

"Aw, honey." Mom gazed sadly at her. "I'm sorry to hear that. Maybe it's just a misunderstanding."

"I doubt it, but it's not all bad. It actually works out great since I need to focus on my writing anyway."

"What happened?"

"Leave the girl alone, Deedee," her father said. "I'm sure Cassie doesn't want to talk about her love life with her mother."

"It's okay, Dad. Mom, we just ended up being too different. It wasn't that great being treated like you were just the girlfriend all the time. It kinda sucks having all your achievements just handed over to someone else who had nothing to do with them just because they are a man."

"Did he make you feel like that?" Her mother picked up her fork and began to eat again. "I never thought he'd be like that. You never can tell with these celebrities, can you?"

"Well, no, he didn't. But everyone else was projecting that on me." *Why did it sound petty now?*

"Then that's not his fault, and you shouldn't make it his." Cassie was surprised that her father had joined the fray. He usually stayed out of things.

Feeling under attack, Cassie pushed her plate away. "He was still acting like a jerk."

"And he might have been. Heck, you don't think your father can be a jerk?"

"Hey!" protested her dad.

"Well, he can be," continued her mother. "But I'm not always innocent either and maybe this time, you aren't as well." She scraped the last of her plate clean. "Now, you can glare at me all you want, Cassandra Pearson, but you can do it from the sink doing the dishes."

Cassie grumbled as she cleared the table. There was no fear of people forgetting her name in this house. Turning the faucet on, she did her best to not think about what her mom had said. She wasn't sure she wanted her parents' advice right now, thank you very much.

THE COZINESS of her apartment wrapped around her like the embrace of an old friend. The padding of her office chair perfectly formed to her behind from long hours of sitting, polishing the words that flowed onto the page. Her notes and paperwork were all neatly in place on trays on her desk. Her open-plan kitchen, dining room, lounge room and work-space all fit into the same footprint as Stirling's ensuite. *Stop thinking about him!*

Cassie furiously scrubbed at her face, as though she could rub the memory of him from her skin. She opened her laptop and looked at the few pages she'd written. Why had she left it so long to write? The threads of the story that had woven together in her mind now felt frayed and worn. Cassie pulled the dog-eared notepad closer, flipping through the flashes of inspiration and the notes that were, more than she'd care to admit, about Stirling. Once they'd made it to Hollywood, she'd tinkered with the plot and the characters, but she'd been too caught up in Stirling, breathing in everything about him while she'd sat in his office, leaving no room in her mind for more.

Cassie picked up a dead leaf that had fallen from her neglected houseplant—maybe she should invest in succulents—turning the desiccated form over and over in her hand until it crumbled to dust. Well, now her mind was clear of all that garbage, thank you very much. The blank page, its white starkness glaring out at her from the screen, taunted her inability to fill it with words. Snapping her laptop shut, she stalked from the room. A shower, that's what she needed. A quick freshen up and then the words would pour from her. Doubt quickened her steps. *At least, I hope they would.*

"AND THEN SHE said she didn't want to talk about it anymore." Freddy's voice rose in astonishment. Frankly, Stirling knew how Bella felt. "If she blooming listened to reason, I wouldn't have to talk about it all the time!"

"Freddy, Bella's a grown woman. She's known her own mind since she was five years old. I'm as tired of hearing it as she is." Stirling slammed his glass down. The occupants of the table beside them cast disapproving looks his way, ones that he returned with his own vaguely threatening glower.

"She's my sister, Stirling. He's hurting her, I know it, and there's nothing I can do about it."

Guilt ratchetted its grip on Stirling. What sort of friend was he to snap at him like that? He reached out a conciliatory hand to clasp Freddy's shoulder. "I'm sorry, Freddy. I know you love her."

"I'm sorry, I know I prattle on about it. Maybe I'll ask Chora to see if she can talk to her again. I know Bella likes her, and maybe this time she'll see sense."

Landon and Chora were flying in from Crete for a baby scan or something that was baby related. Stirling had found his disposition turning sour with thoughts of stubborn writers in red dresses as his friend had been relaying plans for their visit.

He still wasn't sure what had happened in LA with Cassie. One minute he'd felt the most amazing connection he'd ever had with a woman, and the next she was hightailing it out of there and throwing in his face that she didn't like being his girlfriend. Stirling watched Freddy drain his glass. Maybe his friend had the right of it. Free-flowing drinks and a constant stream of women used to be enough. Why had he found a need to change it?

CHORA HAD ALWAYS HAD AN ENERGY. Even Stirling wasn't so self-absorbed that he had been immune to it. Now well into her pregnancy, she might as well be the poster child for motherhood. She fairly glowed, even if she waddled a little.

"Don't smile at me like that," she commanded as she sat down, heaving a sigh of relief once she propped her feet up on the chair diagonally across from her.

He rose and gave her a kiss on the cheek. "You look gorgeous, as usual."

"Like a penguin."

"An adorable mother penguin." He grinned at her. "I'm amazed Landon isn't carrying you around everywhere."

"He'd try to if he thought I would let him. I love that man, but he's getting on my nerves with doing his best to not let me do anything. I'm pregnant, not an invalid. And it's worse when his grandparents are around. They just order the servants to wait on me, and then I tell them I don't want to, and the poor staff almost have a nervous breakdown."

"This baby is very much wanted." Stirling signaled the waiter.

"You have no idea. I'm lucky Landon has a quick meeting at the museum before he is coming to lunch with us. It gives me the chance to find out how you and your lady are doing."

Thankfully the waiter arrived to take their order, saving Stirling from having to answer. Catching the thoughtful way Chora gazed at him, he was confident he wasn't off the hook yet.

She at least had the grace to wait until the attendant had moved away before grilling him. "Spill it, Stirling."

"Cassie and I are on a break."

She blinked, then her eyes narrowed reproachfully. "Why would you do that? Are you stupid? She's fabulous, and I really liked her. Murphy liked her."

"It wasn't my decision, or at least not all my decision." He couldn't even remember how they'd got to this point anymore.

Her expression softened into pity. "Oh, Stirling." She sighed. "What happened?"

"I don't know. I opened everything I had to her"—his home, his wallet, his life, his heart—"and she didn't want it. In fact, her precise words were that she didn't want to be known as Stirling Saint-Claire's girlfriend." *Gosh, it still hurt.*

Chora chewed on the inside of her cheek, her brows scrunched up in thought. "I know I haven't spent as much time with her as you have, but that doesn't seem like the Cassie I met. What was the context around it?"

"She was telling the scriptwriter that when I came in one

day. Actually, she was yelling it at him. And then when I went to see her at a book signing, she mentioned it again." Stirling didn't think Chora had to know how badly he'd acted when he'd gone to the hotel. It wasn't his finest hour.

"What did the scriptwriter say to Cassie to make her say that?"

"I didn't hear that part." He was embarrassed to think he'd never considered what had prompted her reaction other than changes to her work.

"I've been pretty lucky in how I've been treated since I became Landon's wife, and I know you would never make Cassie feel like she's less than you. But the fact remains that society has a way of seeing a woman and, if she's with someone wealthy and powerful, judging her not based on her ability or talent, but on what we assume was given to her by that partner."

"I've never done that to her. All I wanted to do is help." *By being my girlfriend.* Had he created an environment that treated her like that?

Chora held her hand up to silence him. "I'm not saying you did. But Cassie worked for years to carve out a successful career as an author. Do you know how hard that is? Out of all the writers who decide they want to make a living out of it and never do? All those years of self-doubt and hustling to make it happen, and then all of the credit is taken away from her and handed to you?" Chora's empathetic gaze pierced his soul. "Maybe she wasn't angry at you. She was angry with losing her voice, her identity, to just be lumped as Stirling Saint-Claire's girlfriend. You were offended that she didn't want to wear the title with pride, when maybe all she wanted to be is Cassie Pearson, the woman Stirling loves. Tell me, if you lost your identity like that, how would you feel?"

He felt like the pregnant lady across the table from him

had just body-slammed him into the pavement. "I didn't say I loved her."

Knowing eyes smiled kindly back at him. "You didn't have to." She looked past his shoulder. "And with impeccable timing, my husband is here."

Feeling like he'd just run a marathon, he stood once again, this time to greet his best friend. Throughout that long lunch, he found himself time and again returning to thoughts of a feisty bespectacled author who wasn't afraid to speak her mind. *How had he gotten it so wrong?*

CHAPTER 15

"Hello, Cassie." Angie was all professional friendliness. "I hope you're feeling refreshed from your break."

Break? Is that what we're calling it? Cassie stared at the wall above the assistant's head as she fought the urge to turn on her heel and flee from the production office. "It wasn't as long as I'd hoped." *A letter from an attorney had that effect.*

"I know, I feel that way every time I get back from a break to Mexico." Angie glanced down at her screen. "Mr Saint-Claire will see you now."

Mr Saint-Claire will see you now. How things had changed from being able to waltz in whenever she wanted. Heck, she'd always arrived with Stirling, leaving only when he had. "Thanks, Angie, I know the way." Gripping the straps of her handbag tightly, she made her way to Stirling's office with all the enthusiasm of a death row prisoner.

Her treacherous heart beat painfully fast when she saw him seated, immaculately dressed as ever behind his desk. It really was a power position. Only through tremendous willpower did she stop her eyes from drifting to the place on the sofa she'd once occupied. "Hello, Cassie, thank you for coming. I was beginning to think that you had fallen off the face of the planet since you didn't return any of my messages or calls." There was a faint tremor in his voice, like some hidden emotion shook him.

"Well, obviously I didn't fall far enough since your legal representation found me." Cassie pulled the letter from her bag and threw it on his desk. "Nice, real nice, Stirling."

"What would you have me do, Cassie?" He raked his fingers through his hair, leaving it tousled and at odds with the rest of his appearance.

She found herself wanting to smooth it back into place for him. Angered at her own feelings betraying her, she jerked her chin at the offending correspondence. "Obviously threaten me with legal action."

"You were acting like a child and not talking to me."

"No, I was acting like an adult and decided that I had no need for further discourse with you."

"Answered like a true author." He heaved a sigh, lips pressed tightly together before indicating the seat opposite him. "Please sit down, Cassie."

She folded her arms across her chest. "I wasn't planning on staying that long. I have a return flight to Boise to catch this afternoon."

"Sit, Cassie." This time he growled the command. Knees weak, she complied. Satisfied, he smirked at her. "I'm surprised that you aren't interested in continuing to have a say in your movie."

Cassie permitted herself a withering glare. "Like I had a say before. Why don't you just ask Zayne what he thinks the movie needs to be like? He's the one with all the experience, and I'm just the poor, dumb, now ex-girlfriend."

"That's your choice, not mine." His burning eyes held her still. "But since we don't seem to be getting anywhere here, it looks like I'm going to have to do this the hard way." He threw a wire-bound document on the desk, tags of colored paper sticking out from it. "I need to remind you that you are contractually obligated to finish your work on this project. I've highlighted the sections of your contract that applies, if you'd like to read it."

Disbelief that he was actually going to stoop that low stole her breath for a moment. "I don't need to read it."

"Excellent. I've taken the liberty of getting Angie to arrange accommodation for you as you clearly have no wish to return to your previous living arrangements you had in LA." It hung there, heavy in the air between them.

"No."

His eyes hardened, even if the rest of his expression remained blandly pleasant. "Then I look forward to working with you again, Cassie Pearson."

Later as she nursed a glass of wine, staring out from the balcony of her new apartment, she could see Stirling taking a leisurely swim before drying himself off, the towel not hiding his buff physique. The jerk had made sure she was living with a direct view to his mansion. Even when she didn't have to see him for work, he was determined to torture her with not being able to escape his presence.

IT SEEMED that every time Stirling went to check on Cassie, she was urgently needed elsewhere or was just simply somewhere else. He knew she was coming onto the lot each day as he'd had Angie pull up her swipe-in times, but he didn't have personal, concrete, in-the-flesh proof himself.

But today, today was the day he'd finally come up with a plan to coax her out of hiding. He'd come to realize that using a big stick to threaten Cassie into returning to LA might not have given him the outcome he'd wanted when he'd set the plan in motion. *Who knew Cassie Pearson wouldn't like being told what to do?* He smiled at the thought of Little Red being meek. *Never going to happen.* But would he want her to?

Stirling was feeling quite pleased with himself when Angie buzzed through to let him know that Cassie was there. "You wanted to see me?" She didn't take more than two steps into the room.

"Hello, Cassie. You've been quite the challenge to track down." Smirking, he greeted her.

"You forced me to come back here to work, and that's what I'm doing," she ground out, her jaw clenching.

"True, true. Which is why I asked you to come and see me today. There's a meeting that's taking place in a couple of minutes that I would like you to attend with me."

He could see her turning his words around in her mind, looking for any excuse for offense. Frowning, it was obvious she hadn't found any. "Why do you need me to attend it?"

"I didn't say I need you to attend, I said I wanted you to attend," he clarified, enjoying dragging it out. "In fact, you aren't required at all."

"Excellent." Cassie turned sharply on her heel, heading for the door. "Then I'm not going."

"I just thought you might want to sit in on auditions. For your characters."

It was strangely compelling and immensely satisfying watching the internal struggle shake Cassie's slight frame. It was like the two halves of her were fighting for dominance. "It's not like I get a say on who plays them," she finally managed.

"Not final say, no. But your thoughts and comments would go some way to the actors chosen for the roles."

She stilled, and he knew he had her. "Fine. As long as I can veto anyone who is an outright bad fit."

"How about one veto per character?" he bartered.

"Done." She continued to the door. "I'll meet you at the golf cart."

Stirling didn't think *golf cart* had ever sounded so sweet.

"DAVID, this is Cassandra Pearson, and she is the author of this story." Stirling's hand rested lightly in the hollow of Cassie's back. Frankly, he was surprised she hadn't shied away from his touch. Maybe she wasn't as hostile as she'd led him to believe.

"Ms Pearson, pleasure," David greeted.

"Cassie, David is our casting director. Cassie, if you want to sit between us, that way you can give both of us feedback on the actors." Stirling placed his coffee and notepad on the table before taking his own seat.

"Cassie—is it all right if I call you Cassie?" David asked.

"Yes. In fact, I'd prefer it," she said demurely.

"Well, Cassie, there's been quite a bit of interest in this project. In particular, the leading ladies' agents have been inundating me. It's quite the meaty role for these actresses."

"We got a little off course with the script development." Stirling could feel Cassie's sharp gaze piercing him. "But I'm pleased to say we've managed to get it back on track and much closer to the original story as per the book." Her eyes softened, a quizzical frown hovering uncertainly on her brow.

"I think it was the right idea. This script with the right cast and production has Oscar written all over it. Your young lady is quite the talent." David checked his notes. "Now, the first lady we will see is Zoe and..." What followed was a flurry of talent of all shapes and sizes, each hoping to capture the eye of those at the table and get a callback.

And yet, after days, they still had not found the right ones.

"Cassie, did any of them seem right?" David pleaded with her. "It's amazing what makeup and wardrobe can do."

"They just don't have the right manner about them." She shrugged sadly. "Maybe what I have in my head when I wrote them doesn't translate to a real-life actor. Maybe I need to not be a part of this process."

"No, Cassie, you trust your gut instincts," Stirling said firmly. "Let's see how the next one goes." He pressed down on the buzzer. "Can you please send them in." He waited patiently, watching Cassie's face as the actress strode into the room, star quality radiating from every pore.

Cassie's eyes grew huge. "It's Veronica Hughes," she whispered.

"I know. I'm the one who got the script to her agent," he whispered back.

"I hope everything is all right?" Veronica said in her distinct throaty voice. "I'm never sure if whispering is good or bad." She arched a brow imperiously at them.

"I'm so sorry for being rude, Ms Hughes. It's just that, well, I'm a little overwhelmed by the fact that you're here to read for the part," Cassie said, color burning across her cheeks.

"Cassie, I told you I wanted to read the script when you pitched it to me, and I meant it. The role of Agnes is a dream. So much strength, and the struggles she goes through. Even if I hadn't met you, I'd have made my agent get me an audition for it." Stirling thought Cassie might pass out on the spot.

"Veronica, thank you for coming in today. When you're ready." David, reading the situation correctly, took control.

That indescribable X factor, that unknown quality that

made a true star, radiated off Veronica, the merest shift of her facial features or change in body position transforming her into someone else. Stirling watched as she became Agnes in front of their eyes. At the end, he finally managed to pull his eyes away from her to look to Cassie for her reaction. Cassie blinked, wiping a tear from her eye.

"I think we found her. We found our Agnes."

After that, the rest of the major cast fell into place. Vance Killen was to play Jack, Agnes's love interest. Kirk and Ash Cooper were playing the married best friends of Agnes, and Nancy Yi had her first major role as Suki. With a cast like that and the script they had, it was going to be box office gold.

CHAPTER 16

"*I*can't believe they managed to snag Veronica Hughes with a script like that."

Zayne's nasally tones snaked from under the closed door. Stirling stopped, his hand paused in the act of opening said door. *Clearly, Cassie wasn't in there.* Eyes narrowed, he leaned his ear in closer to the door.

"Have you ever read one of Cassandra Pearson's books? I'll save you the pain. It's cheesy, overwritten crap. All about strong women and inspiration." Zayne made a gagging sound. "Please, like that's writing. And then she has the hide to come in here and tell me how to change my script because, excuse me, I'm the writer and these are my characters." He put on a falsetto voice. "Well, excuse me, sweetheart, but the only reason you're here at all is because of whose bed you landed in." Red haze began to descend over Stirling. "Which is another thing. It's not like she's any competition for anything here in LA. Pretty in a plain way, nothing special about her, and now that they've broken up, I don't understand why he keeps letting her have her own way. Maybe that's Stirling thing. He likes them a little vanilla, a little nerdish—" The last word ended in a squeak as Stirling stormed through the door and yanked the phone out of Zayne's stunned hand.

"Zayne has to go right now." He stared at the cowering scriptwriter. "But don't worry, he's about to have a lot of free time on his hands." Stirling hung up and tossed the phone back to its owner. "I'm flattered that you seem so interested in who's in my bed, but Cassie is clearly here on her own merits since she's never been in my bed. I was lucky enough to get her to agree to be my girlfriend for a little while, and there is nothing vanilla about her." *Little Red.* "You're the reason we had to do a script rewrite, and it was that new script that got us Veronica Hughes. The script that was faithful to Cassie's book. Seems to me that Cassie knows more about what makes a good movie than you do." Stirling flipped through the pages of notes on Zayne's desk. "But it's not too late for you. Go away, work hard on your craft, and maybe at some point your instincts will be as good as hers." He tossed the last paper back disdainfully. "And oh, you're fired from this and all of my future projects. I wouldn't be surprised if word gets around and you suddenly find yourself unemployable."

Zayne's face blanched. "You can't do that," he blustered, fat jowls wobbling like an irate turkey.

Stirling looked down at his nails, enjoying the moment immensely. "I can and I have. If you aren't out of here in five minutes, security will escort you from the studio lot. Imagine how embarrassing that will be for your reputation." He slapped his palm on the desk, causing Zayne to jerk back in alarm. "Make sure you leave all of your security passes on your way out, too."

Whistling softly in a low menacing tone of pure satisfaction, he went in search of Cassie.

"Cassie, I hope you don't mind that I got your number from Stirling." Chora's voice was pure sunshine down the line.

"Not at all, it's nice to hear from you." Uncertain at why Chora was calling, Cassie fidgeted with her pen, staring at the last words she'd written. *The billionaire whispered into the lady in red's ear...*

"I'm so glad to hear that you feel that way. I was just talking to Murphy the other day about how much we'd love to catch up with you, and I think I have the perfect excuse to make that happen. I'm going to send out official invites, but I'd love it if you could come to my baby shower."

Cassie was touched to be included, and she was fairly certain that Chora didn't have to invite her just to make up numbers. She had that sort of light-up-the-room personality that she was sure to have people lining up around the block for an invite. "But, um." Cassie hesitated. "You know that Stirling and I aren't together anymore, right?"

"He mentioned something like that, but I'm inviting you because I think we could be friends. Look, I know I've put you on the spot. I'll send over the invitation, and you can think about it and let me know."

She really was a nice person. "Thank you, and thanks for thinking to invite me. It's been a little rough the last couple of weeks."

"Nothing that a few glasses of wine with the girls won't cure." Chora giggled. "Well, sparkling grape juice for me."

"I'll drink your wine for you."

"I'm going to hold you to that. I'd better get going. Landon's in the kitchen and there's the most amazing smells coming from there. I wonder if he's been watching YouTube videos again."

"You'd best investigate." Smiling happily, Cassie hung up

the phone. It would be fun to catch up with Chora and Murphy again. But would it be awkward now that she wasn't with Stirling?

"Can I hope that smile is for me?" Stirling filled the doorway, his hip resting against the frame looking sexy as all heck.

Pushing away the feelings that threatened to overwhelm her, she stared coolly back at him. Being neutral around him was the best policy. "Chora just rang."

"She likes you."

"Oh, did she say something to you?"

"When I saw her last. You made quite the impression on her, and she's a good judge of people."

Flustered, she stared back down at the words written in front of her. "Oh, um, is there something you wanted from me?" she asked, half in dread, half in anticipation.

"Well, to start with, it's been a lot easier to find you since the auditions." His voice was soft and intimate.

"It was tiring making myself hard to find." And yet she'd always hoped he'd find her.

"I owe you an apology."

Her lips parted in surprise. "You do?" she squeaked. Recovering, she said more firmly, "You do."

"I overheard Zayne saying some things, and you were right. I should have listened to you about him. I should have supported you, my girlfriend, not sided with him because of something I thought I heard which, as it turns out, was all out of context. He won't be a problem anymore. I fired him."

"No, it shouldn't have had anything to do with if I was your girlfriend or not. You should have known me better. But you threw it back in my face about how you knew best, and you didn't." It still hurt thinking about it. But she wasn't his girlfriend anymore. She'd regained her independence, her sense of self. "Stirling, we started out in a fake relationship pretending we knew each other. My mistake was forgetting that just because we ended up being in a real relationship, it still didn't mean we knew each other." It hit her hard, the truth of her own words. She loved this man, but she didn't know him any better than he knew her and she sure as heck wasn't cut out to be just the girlfriend. "I don't even blame you. I got caught up in the fantasy of it all. The fact is, I began to start believing my own story. As far as Zayne goes, I fought him hard and ended up with the script that my book deserved, but it only happened because I didn't quietly do what was expected and go sit in the corner, and that's no thanks to you. You only supported me when I left and then tried to show how you were listening to me when you forced me to come back." She sighed like it would somehow ease the pressure in her chest. "Maybe I'm starting to know you after all. Now, if you haven't got anything else to add, I'm done talking. I'd like to be alone."

They stared across at each other in a sudden ringing silence before, without another word, Stirling pushed himself off the frame and stalked away, taking the remnants of her heart with him.

CHAPTER 17

*I*t was odd how an inanimate object could somehow take on the mood of its cargo. Stirling's private jet was filled with all the bourgeoisie trappings his family would despise. It wasn't, after all, terribly British to flaunt one's wealth like the nouveau riche. Frankly, Stirling didn't give two hoots about convention. He liked to surround himself with bright, shiny things. Maybe that was why Hollywood had always been such a good fit for him. *What a time for self-reflection.*

Sharing it with Cassie had added an extra dimension to the jet. Her unabashed enjoyment of the finer things in life, her somehow childlike appreciation, had made it seem that much better. Like Christmas morning when you were privileged to see it through the innocent eyes of a child after years of jaded adulthood. His thoughts finally returned to where he was sitting in the club with his friends.

"So, how was the trip over, old chap?" Freddy drawled.

"From the looks Cassie gave Stirling when he stopped by to say hello to Chora, I would say positively frigid." Landon chuckled, not the least bit intimidated by the hostile glare Stirling sent his way.

"I never thought I would see the day that Stirling Saint-Claire couldn't bloody buy or talk his way out of a woman's bad books." Alistair sighed dramatically. "It's a sad day for men all over the world—the fall of such a hero."

"I never thought you two clowns would be happily married, and yet here we are," snapped Stirling.

"Touchy, aren't you, old sport? If I didn't know better, I'd think they'd hit a nerve." Freddy winked over the brim of his crystal tumbler to his friends. "One called Cassie Pearson."

"He has it bad," Landon agreed.

"Has what?" Stirling signaled for another round of drinks. Changing his mind, he gestured for them to just leave the bottle.

"Poor chap's still in denial." Freddy shook his head sadly.

"I'm not in blooming denial, and like you'd know anything about being in a relationship," Stirling growled. *They could all bloody well shove off with their smugly superior attitudes—especially Freddy.*

"And there's the next stage—anger," Alistair noted sagely. "He has it bad."

"I don't know what you lot are talking about." Stirling caught himself hunching his shoulders defensively around his drink. Quickly, he thrust them back, raising his chin to stare each of them defiantly in the eyes.

"Are you really going to play that game with us?" Landon asked, pouring himself another drink. "Have you told her you love her yet?"

The smooth whiskey turned violent in his throat, searing as he coughed and spluttered, tears coming to his eyes as the alcohol vapors frolicked in his esophagus. "Why would I do a thing like that?"

"Because it's true." Alistair thumped him helpfully on the

back. "I know it doesn't make it any less painful to admit, but it is true."

"It doesn't matter if it's true or not." Stirling wiped at his stinging eyes, thankful that breathing didn't hurt anymore.

"Why?" Landon skewered him with a gaze that saw through his protests.

"Because she doesn't want to hear it. Are you happy now?" Why wouldn't his friends just let it drop?

"Never met a woman who didn't want to hear it, even if it wasn't the truth," Freddy sniggered.

"Oh, shut up, Freddy. Like I'm going to take advice from you." Stirling cast daggers at his smirking friend.

"In this case, he's right." Landon took another sip from the amber liquid in his glass. "Especially since, in your case, it's true."

Stirling could quite happily throttle all his smug, smirking friends. *Who needs friends like them anyway? Especially the happily married ones. They were the worst of all.*

"So, here are the rules," Misty said, rubbing hands gleefully together as she got down to business in a room festooned with balloons, streamers, and all things baby. "Each of you will get two of these dummies to wear around your neck."

Cassie nodded. It seemed simple enough. Chora's friend seemed very focused on everyone knowing what was going on.

"Each time someone says baby, you lose a dummy. Once you lose them all, you're out of the game." Misty eyed the group. "Any questions?"

"I don't have any dummies," Kelly said from the TV screen

they'd hooked up for the teleconference. Being heavily pregnant herself, flying had been quite out of the question.

"Do you have the package I sent you and told you not to open until I said so?" Misty asked, peering into the TV like she could somehow find it herself.

"Yes." Kelly grabbed at something just out of shot.

"Then open it." Misty settled herself back down on the sofa.

"Oh, there are dummies in here. Never mind." Kelly giggled. "I won't tell you what else is in here yet. I wouldn't want to ruin the surprise."

"Is Misty always so…" Cassie wasn't entirely sure how to finish her question without offending the other woman.

"Such a force of nature?" Evelyn, another of Chora's friends, supplied helpfully.

"Focused?" Chora's lips quirked.

"Would run you over if you got between her and her goal?" Murphy stretched her legs out before crossing them over at the ankle.

"You should have seen her before she married Logan. He's calmed her down somewhat." Evelyn grinned at her friend. "Before that, she was wound a little tight."

If this was the calm Misty, Cassie wasn't sure she had the stamina for the high energy one.

"I wish Bella had decided to come. I see her less and less now, and I know it's all because of her boyfriend. Poor Freddy is beside himself with worry about his sister. Oh!" Chora gave a little gasp, rubbing at her belly.

"Is everything all right? Was it the baby?" Evelyn leaned forward, eyes wide.

"What's going on with the baby?" Kelly asked through the screen.

"Just a little kick, nothing to worry about." Chora

scrunched her face up. "But I could do without all the elbows the baby keeps throwing.

"Hand them over." Misty held her hand out for the dummies, snapping her fingers.

"Oh, man, really? I'm losing one already?" Evelyn groaned. "I thought I would last a little longer than that before I lost one."

"I blame the lag. I wasn't sure what was going on." Kelly stared at them from the wall. "Now I feel all jittery. I don't want to be the first person to get kicked out of the game"

Cassie picked up a rainbow frosted cupcake from the display in front of her. She was enjoying herself immensely. After suffering through the flight here with Stirling after he'd insisted she travel with him and refusing to take no for an answer, it was nice to be surrounded by the friendship these women shared. And they were generous. Not once did she feel like she wasn't included in the warmth of the room.

"How have you been, Cassie? I really appreciate you taking the trouble to fly over." Chora smiled kindly at her, a wealth of understanding shining out from her warm gaze.

Cassie felt herself tear up from that look. "I'm glad I came. I mean, the flight I could've done without, but it's worth it now that I'm here."

"Was the flight bad? Did you have turbulence?" Evelyn asked, biting into her own cupcake.

Chora and Murphy pulled silencing faces, Evelyn frowning at them, trying to figure out what faux pas she was making. "Um?"

"It's okay, guys." Cassie shrugged. "It's not like it's a secret. I flew over with Stirling, who was my pretend boyfriend turned real boyfriend turned ex-boyfriend."

"I can see why she's the romance writer. I'd definitely buy this story," Misty whispered to Evelyn.

"I was sorry to hear you'd broken up," Murphy said. "It's

like I told Alistair, if ever there was a bloody woman who could keep Stirling from being too big-headed, it was you."

Cassie scrunched up her face. "Ah, thank you, I think?"

"Why did you break up?" Misty asked.

"It's complicated."

"I find people have a tendency to try to make things more complicated than they have to be, when it's really quite simple." Kelly's voice sounded weird in surround sound. "Do you love him?"

"It doesn't matter." Her heart clenched as pain spasmed through her.

"I think it does, but why do you think it doesn't matter?" Kelly was clearly not letting it go.

Cassie sighed. She might as well throw it all out there. Maybe then Kelly would let it go and they could get back to enjoying the baby shower. "Because we kinda fell into a relationship before we knew each other and somehow I lost my identity along the way. Plus, he doesn't love me."

"Girl," Misty said, waving Cassie's protests aside. "Love is messy. Like, gloriously undiluted slop, and I know what I speak of when I say that."

"She really does," agreed Evelyn. *There had to be some kind of story behind that comment.*

"Even if you know each other, it's a mess. And who you are, it changes, it grows, it's not some sort of stagnant being." Misty pushed on, warming to her subject.

"And I happen to know Stirling is in love with you." Chora threw the cat amongst the pigeons with her pronouncement.

"Excuse me, what?" Cassie choked on the crumbs of her cupcake. How could sugar turn on her like this?

"Yes, he told me when I spoke to him a while ago." Chora calmly took a sip of tea from a delicate bone china cup, completely undisturbed by the furor she had caused while looking like a pregnant Madonna.

"Maybe you heard wrong." Cassie's heart froze and then spasmed to life, the news sending it pounding.

"No, we talked about it at length. He loves you, even if he hasn't quite put all the pieces together yet." Chora's lips quirked. "And from where I'm sitting, you love him."

A sob escaped from Cassie. "I don't love him, and it's all a mess, and now I'm ruining your baby shower."

Chora and Murphy exchanged amused glances. "Would it hurt so much if you didn't?" Murphy asked.

"And don't worry about my baby shower. Once you fall in love with one of these boys, it makes us family." Chora took off her remaining dummy and handed it over to Misty. "And just like that, I'm the first one out of the game at my own party." She grinned at Cassie. "You'd better hand yours over too."

Cassie complied, only half listening to the chatter around her. Did she love him? Was Murphy right? Was that why it hurt so much?

CHAPTER 18

"Are you sure you know what you're doing, old chap?" Freddy peered out from the back of the town car to the mansion in front of them.

"Of course he bloody does." Alistair clapped Stirling on the shoulder. "You do know what you're doing, right, mate?"

"If we stick to the plan, we'll be fine." Stirling wiped his sweaty palms on his trousers, his emerald-eyed panther cufflinks snagging on the fabric. "What could go wrong?"

"Are you daft, man?" Landon demanded incredulously. "There's a houseful of women between you and your prize. Those odds aren't in your favor."

"It's a chance I'm willing to take." Stirling cracked the car door open. "Who's with me?"

"The brave fool," whispered Alistair, sliding across the back seat to open his door.

"But what a way to go—in a houseful of women." Freddy followed suit. "I can't decide if that's heaven or hell."

"Purgatory?" Landon suggested, poking his head back into the car. "Now, if you girls are finished chatting, we have a job to do."

"Keep your trousers on, old sport. I'm right behind you."

Stirling eyed the lit windows of the mansion, silhouettes moving about. "Ready or not, Little Red, I'm coming for you."

His friends gathered beside him like soldiers ready to go into battle. "We'll get you to your girl, but what happens after that is up to you," Landon said before striding forward. "And just remember, my wife's pregnant. I don't want anything upsetting her."

"Because storming into your own house and disrupting her baby shower isn't going to bloody upset her at all," Alistair muttered.

"You can talk. I'm not sure I'd want to deal with your wife when she's angry. Not only can she rope and tie up cattle, but she also knows how to castrate them," Landon threw over his shoulder.

"Ouch." Freddy winced. "Are you listening to this, Stirling? Are you sure you want to do this?" He hustled to keep up with the others.

"More than anything." Stirling almost slammed into the back of Landon as he stopped at the door. "What are you doing?"

"Excuse me if I don't want to actually break into my own house," Landon hissed over his shoulder.

"Just use your key," Stirling whispered back.

Landon's face reddened as his gaze dropped to his feet. "I might have forgotten it."

"Are you serious? What sort of mission have I signed up for?" Freddy reached over and pressed the doorbell. "And I'm not even the brains of this operation. Let that sink in for a minute."

Laughter gurgled up in Stirling. It was all so absurd, and yet here he was. And all because of Cassie. A snort bubbled out his nose.

"Don't you bloody start," Alistair blustered. "I swear, if you do, I'm going to lose it over here."

A snigger escaped from Landon. "You have to admit, this is a first for us."

Freddy was the first to crack under pressure, a great geyser of mirth exploding from him, sucking everyone into its chortling vortex. The butler was a credit to his profession and superior training and didn't even flinch in the face of such hilarity.

"My lord, I wasn't expecting you back so early. My lady is with her guests, preparing to head out to a light supper."

"Stand back, Winston, there's no time." Landon pushed past him and strode down the hall, his friends at his heels, before he slammed to a stop. "Um, which room are they in?"

"They are gathering in the drawing room, but I believe not all of the guests are there yet."

"Excellent. And Winston?"

"Yes, my lord?"

"I think it's best you make yourself scarce. This evening is about to become epic." Landon swaggered as he resumed his way forward. "And yes, I just said epic."

"What the bloody heck is going on here?" Murphy appeared, hands on hips. "Chora's going to kill you if you ruin her baby shower, Landon."

"I'll deal with Chora." Landon made to sidestep her, but Murphy was too quick and blocked his way. Looking over his shoulder her eyes narrowed. "Alistair, what's going on?"

Alistair rested a hand on his friend's shoulder. "It's time we come clean."

"The blazes it is," muttered Freddy, ready to charge.

Stirling shook his head in warning. Alistair walked up to his wife, smiling tenderly into her eyes. "You look beautiful."

Her expression didn't change. "It's going to take more than that."

Quickly, Alistair threw his by now swearing wife over his shoulder and, with a few firm swipes to her bottom, made off down the hall.

"Remember the cattle, old chap," Freddy called after the departing couple.

"Okay, that's one down. We still have, by my count, three more before Stirling is clear to get to Cassie. Let's go." Landon led the way forward again.

A blonde head and a dark head popped out from over the banister of the staircase. "You're early!" the blonde woman hissed.

Stirling looked at Landon and Freddy and shrugged. *What was going on?*

"Do you need to get changed? I like a sharply dressed man in a suit as much as the next woman, but it's not what I ordered for Chora. And Landon, you should've told me they'd arrived. What if Chora sees?" she continued. "And did you need to bring a posse? Just the one I ordered is suffice."

"I still don't get why you ordered a stripper for a baby shower, Misty." The dark-haired woman turned to her friend. "It's not exactly traditional."

"Nothing Chora's done is traditional, and she skipped giving me the opportunity to give her a hens party. So, this is the next best thing, Evelyn."

Freddy swaggered forward. "He's my apprentice, still learning the ropes on how to give a woman what she wants." *Why was he making his voice so deep? And was that an American accent he was trying?*

"Here he goes," groaned Landon.

"If you lovely ladies can show me where to get changed, I'll leave the lad to cool his heels down there." Freddy turned, smirking to the boys. "I've got this, since it appears I'm the only one who has the physique to pull off being a stripper."

With light steps, he danced up the stairs, the women pulling their heads back out of sight.

Stirling was beginning to feel like the sketchy plan they'd begun their escapade with was spiraling out of his control. "Let's go before they get a good look at him and demand a refund."

Landon chuckled. "It's what I'd do."

The last few yards of the hall somehow seemed both panic-inducingly short and painfully long. As Landon pushed the door open, Stirling could hear muffled voices. More than he'd anticipated, given the headcount Landon had supplied them with. Baffled, he followed his friend into the room and stopped, halted by a vision in a red dress.

CASSIE STARED OPENMOUTHED at the men barging into the sanctuary of the drawing room. "Good evening, Landon and Stirling," Kelly greeted from the television on the wall. Although she wouldn't be able to attend the restaurant, she'd still be able to chat with them as they had pre-dinner drinks.

Landon marched over to the table and picked up the remote. "Hello, Kelly. I know this is going to be terribly rude, but I need to turn you off now."

"What?" Chora demanded, her eyes wide in horror as her hand rested on her extended belly. "I don't think so. Not at my baby shower."

Cassie stared up at the television screen aghast at what was happening. *Actually, what was happening? Why was Landon being rude, or even here? And why was Stirling skulking in the doorway?*

"My darling wife is needed elsewhere, and as soon as she's finished, I'm sure she will be straight on the phone to apologize for my appalling behavior and let you in on everything that's happened." Landon scooped Chora up off the sofa, remote still in hand.

"I'm intrigued now. Goodnight to all." The screen went blank as Kelly's curious face disappeared.

"Landon Astley! I swear, if you don't start telling me what the heck is going on, I'll—" Chora's face looked like she was ready to explode, which is something no one wants in a pregnant lady.

"Calm down." *Like saying that to someone ever worked.* Landon planted a kiss on his love's nose and whispered something in her ear. Whatever it was stopped her squirming to get free.

"This better work." She pulled his face closer to hers. "Otherwise, I'm going to be very upset with you."

"I have complete confidence." Landon smiled at Stirling as Chora beamed at Cassie and, with a gentle wave in their direction, they left the room, Stirling closing the door softly behind them.

"Um, well, I guess I should be going, too." Cassie set her glass down on the coffee table before rising to her feet.

"Not after I went to all this trouble to get you alone." Despite his closed expression, she could sense a vulnerability to him.

Her heart ached. How had they gotten to this point? "Oh." Her legs turning to jelly, she sunk back down again.

"Did you ever wonder why I gave you the power to rewrite the script?"

Cassie felt foolish. He wanted to talk about work. "Because you wanted to get back in my good graces?"

His lips quirked. "Maybe that was a bonus. But I bought the rights to your book because you're a brilliant writer. It didn't need to be changed. It was perfect how it was. And you, Cassandra Pearson, are perfect as you are."

Something mended in her heart as he gazed at her. "I

wrote a lot of things about you when I was taking notes. Not all of them are particularly flattering in the beginning. To be honest, I was shaping you up to be the villain of the story." She shrugged sadly. "Like I'd somehow made you in my head for my real-life story with you." Cassie stared down at her hands. "But when it became time to write it, somehow you always turned out to be the hero my heroine needed."

"You actually wrote about me? All those times I asked, I was only teasing." Stirling walked slowly across the room toward her until he had her hands tenderly clasped in his own. The warmth of them flowed through her palms to her heart. She was shocked by the impact of his gentle touch.

"Yes."

"What exactly did you write?"

Cassie tried to ignore the strange ache in her limbs. "I can't tell you. I haven't finished it yet. So you'll have to wait like everyone else and buy the book." Mischievousness made her raise her brow at him. "Or maybe watch the movie, if they make one, but it doesn't have an option on it yet."

Stirling's hand went to the nape of her neck, both intoxicating and calming her. "I think I might know someone who might be able to take care of that."

"Yeah?"

"Yeah. Cassie Pearson's boyfriend."

"She already had a pretend boyfriend who became a real boyfriend and then she lost her own identity and, to be honest, she didn't handle it well at all."

"I've been thinking that maybe we need to spend more time getting to know everything about each other, and I'm willing to spend the rest of my life doing just that." Stirling breathed deeply. "I love you, Little Red, and one day I want to marry you. But I'm convinced that even if I do get to spend the rest of my life with you, it still won't be enough time to learn everything I want to know about you." He smiled, gazing deeply into her eyes. "Maybe I'll need two lifetimes just to make sure I do it right. I love you, and if you'll let me, I'd like to be Cassandra Pearson's boyfriend again." He slipped the diamond encrusted panther bracelet from his pocket and onto the wrist it belonged. "Matching again," he said as he spied the emerald eyes gleaming from his own wrists. "Now, how about the boyfriend thing?"

Cassie sniffled. Gosh, she loved this man. "Only if I get to introduce you as that to everyone. Maybe get Angie to send out an email?"

"I think we can arrange that." With a light pressure on the back of her neck, he pulled her closer until their foreheads touched. "Does that mean I've been accepted as the arm candy for the famous romance author?"

"I think we can arrange it." She breathed him in like he was the elixir of life. "I love you, Stirling."

"Thank goodness. Because after putting this plan into action, there wasn't really a plan B. Frankly, I'm not even sure if Freddy hasn't been arrested yet."

She jerked back a little. "What?"

Grinning, he pulled her back in. "Don't worry, he can afford bail." Before she could protest more, his lips drove away all other thoughts.

The heroine was pulled snuggly into the arms of her love, letting the last of her doubts—now as insubstantial as mist in the breeze—dissolve. Theirs was a love that was only beginning, but what an adventure it would be...

EPILOGUE

Freddy sat on the stairs. Stirling had swept Cassie out the door and into a waiting town car, no doubt back to his mansion to whisper sweet nothings in her ear and make sappy plans for the future. Landon was in the drawing room with Chora, Alistair and Murphy. From the open door, he could see his friend's arm snug around his pregnant wife, from time to time kissing her tenderly on the head as he spoke to the couple across from them.

Murphy's legs were draped over her husband's, flashing him a quick smile before continuing on with her story, Alistair content to lean back and wrap himself around her. Upstairs he could hear more laughter from the two women he'd met—Misty and Evelyn—no doubt to the husbands he'd heard all about.

Freddy glanced down at the now-empty tumbler he'd snagged earlier. All this marital happiness was enough to drive a man to drink.

"A refill?" Winston appeared on silent feet offering a fresh crystal decanter.

A tremor ran through Freddy's hand as more laughter wafted around them. "Old chap, I'm going to need something stronger than that."

"I don't believe there's anything stronger in the house." Winston sniffed, offended that somehow his hospitality should be found wanting.

"That's quite all right, Winston. It's not your fault that you aren't running a gaming den from the kitchen, but I know somewhere that is." Pushing himself languidly off the stairs, he brushed himself down. "If you would be so kind as to call a town car for me, it's time I left the married people to do boring old married people things." Freddy leaned into Winston, the butler wincing either from the overfamiliar gesture or the alcohol fumes on his breath. "They can't all be free-living bachelors like you and me. As wild and untamed as the wind, we are."

"Quite right, my lord." *Was there a hint of a smile on the man's staid face?*

"A word of advice. I'd take to wearing a face mask around them. Until we find a cure—or the very least, a vaccination—you can't be too careful not to catch what they have." With one final soulful look, Freddy released him, making his way unsteadily down the hall. Somewhere out there in the foggy London night, there was a poker match or a baccarat game or even dice that had his name on it. *Better not keep it waiting.*

THE END

As an Indie Author, reviews help me get my books noticed. If you enjoyed reading Stirling's and Cassie's story as much as I did writing it, please leave a review. It will make all the difference to me.

If you loved, *Star Dust and the Billionaire,* sign up for my newsletter here to get free bonus's and exclusive news. Now, turn the page to discover Freddy's story, *Gold Dust and the Billionaire*

SNEAK PEEK – GOLD DUST AND THE
BILLIONAIRE

Freddy kept his gaze steady on the cards in front of him. Inside he felt like his innards were vibrating. The men who sat around the table all had the veneer of social, genial gentlemen, but he knew they were ruthless. The big man in the corner of the room had a memorandum book with names and numbers and he always got what was owed, one way or another.

But not tonight. Tonight, the gods smiled down on him, and he'd come up trumps. "Silvio, are you going to meet or fold?" Freddy tried to keep his voice coolly casual. A bead of sweat broke out on Silvio's forehead. With his baldness and pale fleshiness, it was hard to not liken him to a nervous boiled egg. Freddy rather liked eating them for breakfast. He knew his friends would be surprised to hear the ruthlessness of his thoughts. They, after all, were quite often of the mind to think of him as lackadaisical and without ambition. Fact was, he had plenty, just no clue what to do with it. "Silvio? What is the saying? Poop or get off the pot."

Silvio spun the thick gold ring on his index finger with his thumb. "I've got nothing left to meet with, except…" He ran a hand over his head. "I have a horse. I bought it for my wife."

"I didn't know your wife rides." Freddy had seen pictures of the wife in society pages, and he felt a sudden pity for the beast for having to lug her gargantuan frame about.

"She doesn't. There's a girl who rides him. Sally just goes to the events as his owner and gets to keep the prizes."

"Seems … sporting."

"The horse is fully imported, bloodlines in the purple, and a stallion. Worth a bomb, and from what my wife tells me, wins everything it enters. I'm adding the horse to the wager."

Freddy quirked a brow at him, running his nail over the edge of his cards. "You're offering me a racehorse?"

"Not a racehorse. A warmblood. One that does dressage."

"A horse is a horse, I guess. Fine, I accept. Throw it in the pot." A trill of anticipation made his senses sharpen. "Now, show your hand."

Mutely, with a gleam of triumph, Silvio revealed his straight flush.

"I do like a flush myself," Freddy murmured as he turned his cards. "Personally, I find a royal flush much more satisfying." Silvio gaped at him, revealing yellowing teeth. "Now, what's my new horse called?"

Gold Dust and the Billionaire available on Amazon and in Kindle Unlimited here

ACKNOWLEDGMENTS

A debt of gratitude to my editor Rebekah Groves for her patience with me.

Another big thanks to Megan from Designed with Grace for her cover design.

To my amazing beta readers and street team, you guys rock and I couldn't do it without you.

And finally to my fabulous alpha reader Trixie Norman, for all the late nights of reading and endless questions about your thoughts.

Red Dust and The Billionaire

Wild horses couldn't drag this couple to happily ever after…right?

Pre Order Now

Star Dust and The Billionaire

Buy Now

Gold Dust and The Billionaire

Freddy's Story Coming Soon…

Pre Order Now

Cowboy Christmas Series

<u>The Mistletoe Collection</u>

Boots and Mistletoe

Cowboy boots, mistletoe, and a holiday do-over…

Buy Now

The Cowboy Under the Mistletoe

It'll take more than the magic of the season to help this grump find her happily ever after…

Buy Now

Mistletoe and the Billionaire's Cowgirl

He's the last man she wants this holiday season. Too bad he's exactly what she needs…

Buy Now

Barrels and Hearts series

Available on Amazon and Kindle Unlimited

A Bull Rider's Paradise

The prequel to the Barrels and Hearts series. True love is only the beginning….of the story. Find out where it all began with Ana and Eduardo. Sometimes finding love is easy. It's keeping it that's hard.

Buy here

A Cowgirl's Dream

An Aussie cowgirl far from home. A handsome Brazilian bull rider. Can they have a rodeo love story of their dreams?

Buy Now

A Cowgirl's Heart

An Aussie cowgirl in need. Her childhood friend to the rescue. Can friendship turn into a love story?

Buy Now

A Cowgirl's Passion

One feisty cowgirl. One steadfast Brazilian bull rider. Will she see what is right in front of her?

Buy Now

A Cowgirl's Pride

An Aussie cowgirl from the wrong side of the tracks. A handsome equine vet. Can they find a way to have their happy ever after?

Buy Now

A Cowgirl's Love

A young Aussie cowgirl. A widowed rancher. Does age matter when it comes to love?

Buy Now

A Cowgirl's Movie Star

A fiery cowgirl with big dreams. A movie star far from home. When their two worlds collide, will their love be strong enough to hold them together or will they be pulled apart

Buy Now

A Cowgirl's Billionaire

A cowgirl adrift. A broken billionaire cowboy. Can he free himself from the past to be the man she needs now?

Buy Now

ABOUT THE AUTHOR

Edith MacKenzie or Eddie Mac to her friends is an author of sweet and wholesome contemporary cowboy romance. They say in literary circles to write what you know, and Eddie has certainly taken that to heart. Before embarking on a writing career, she trained horses professionally and brings that wealth of knowledge to her writing.

Now a mum to a boy and girl, as well as wife, she delights with her tales of strong cowgirls and their adventures in finding love. When not weaving the love stories of her characters, she enjoys hanging out with her family and animals, as well as reading, fishing and camping.

Just remember—once a cowgirl, always a cowgirl.

facebook.com/EddieMacAuthor
instagram.com/edith_mackenzie_author
amazon.com/Edith-MacKenzie
bookbub.com/profile/edith-mackenzie
twitter.com/edith_mackenzie